HAS ONE OF THE BIGGEST THOROUGHBRED RACES OF THE YEAR BEEN FIXED?

Carole hurried forward and knelt down in front of the goat that was company for the expensive racehorse, Monkeyshines. "Are you feeling all right, Blackie?" she asked, scratching his head between the hard little horns. On a hunch, she leaned over and picked up the slightly soggy mouthful of hay the goat had dropped. She examined it for a second, then jumped to her feet. "Hey, you guys! Look at this," she exclaimed. "This hay is moldy through and through!"

Stevie and Lisa hurried over to see for themselves. "You're right," Stevie said with a low whistle. "No wonder Blackie didn't want to eat this. It would have made him sick as—"

"Monkeyshines!" Carole interrupted her. She rushed off down the aisle. "If Blackie stole it from Monk's stall, there might be more. We have to get it before he does—if we're not already too late!"

THE SADDLE CLUB

PHOTO FINISH

BONNIE BRYANT

A SKYLARK BOOK
NEW YORK · TORONTO · LONDON · SYDNEY · AUCKLAND

RL 5, 009–012

PHOTO FINISH

A Bantam Skylark Book / April 1995

Skylark Books is a registered trademark of Bantam Books,
a division of Bantam Doubleday Dell Publishing Group, Inc.
Registered in U.S. Patent and Trademark Office and elsewhere.

"The Saddle Club" is a trademark of Bonnie Bryant Hiller.
The Saddle Club design / logo, which consists of
a riding crop and a riding hat, is a
trademark of Bantam Books.

ISBN 0-553-48261-0

Published simultaneously in the United States and Canada

Bantam Books are published by Bantam Books, a division of Bantam Doubleday Dell Publishing Group, Inc. Its trademark, consisting of the words "Bantam Books" and the portrayal of a rooster, is Registered in U.S. Patent and
Trademark Office and in other countries. Marca Registrada. Bantam Books,
1540 Broadway, New York, New York 10036.

PRINTED IN THE UNITED STATES OF AMERICA

OPM   0   9   8   7   6   5   4   3   2   1

I would like to express my
special thanks to Catherine Hapka
for her help in the writing
of this book.

"WAIT, HOLD IT there, just for another second," Lisa Atwood called out, fiddling with the focus on her camera. "That's it. . . ."

Lisa and her two best friends, Carole Hanson and Stevie Lake, were in the outdoor ring at Pine Hollow Stable, where they all took riding lessons. It was Saturday afternoon, and their lessons were over for the day. Most of the other riders had already gone home, but Lisa, Carole, and Stevie hadn't even untacked their horses yet. That's because Lisa had asked her friends to pose for her while she took pictures with her new camera.

Carole, Stevie, and Lisa loved riding—and each other —so much that they'd started a group called The Saddle Club. The Saddle Club had only two basic requirements. The first was that all members had to be horse crazy. The second was that members had to be willing to help one another with anything at any time, horse related or otherwise.

What Lisa was asking The Saddle Club to help her with now wasn't very difficult. But it *was* getting a little boring. Lisa had recently started taking a photography class after school, and she loved it. Her mother was thrilled to see her taking such a strong interest in something other than horses. Lisa had started riding lessons at Mrs. Atwood's insistence, since according to Mrs. Atwood riding was something a proper young lady ought to be able to do, along with playing tennis, the piano, and countless other things. But Mrs. Atwood had never expected her daughter to become horse crazy, and Lisa knew her mother didn't quite approve. They had reached an understanding on the topic, but Mrs. Atwood still couldn't help looking for ways to encourage Lisa's other interests. And the way she'd decided to encourage her interest in photography was by buying her a brand-new, very fancy and complicated camera.

In the week since she'd gotten the camera, Lisa had taken pictures of everything she could think of—her friends, her house, her dog, and especially Pine Hollow's horses. She already had dozens of pictures of the horse she usually rode, a pretty Thoroughbred named Prancer. She also had plenty of pictures of Carole's horse, Starlight, and Stevie's horse, Belle. And she had taken numerous pictures of Topside, Comanche, Diablo, Barq,

Delilah, Calypso, Nero, Harry, Romeo, Tecumseh, Dapper, Samson, Patch, Rusty, Chippewa, Garnet, Bluegrass, Geronimo, Nickel, Dime, Quarter, and every other horse and pony at Pine Hollow. She had pictures of them eating. She had pictures of them sleeping. She had pictures of them jumping, walking, running, and trotting. She had pictures of them being groomed.

And Carole and Stevie had been there for most of them.

Now Lisa was looking for new and more interesting ways to photograph the horses. At the moment, Stevie and Belle, a mischievous bay mare, were pretending to be circus performers. Stevie was standing balanced in her left stirrup. Her right leg was stretched out to the side, and her left arm rose above her head in a dramatic pose. Riding that way took a lot of balance, strength, and concentration even though Belle was moving at a slow, smooth walk. Even for a good rider like Stevie, it wasn't easy.

"That's it!" Lisa cried excitedly. She moved her hand away from the zoom lens just a little too fast. "Oh, nuts!" she exclaimed as her finger hit the lens and jarred it out of focus again. She frantically refocused as Stevie tried desperately to hold her position.

Unfortunately, Belle had other ideas. She was tired of the pose, and seized with a sudden urge to graze. She stopped abruptly near the fence and lowered her head, snuffling at the dusty ground in search of stray tufts of grass. As the reins pulled her forward, Stevie slid to one side and nearly lost her balance. She managed to grab a handful of mane and started wiggling her foot around, searching for the stirrup. But then Belle quickly decided that she'd have better luck finding grass somewhere else. She moved off at a trot toward the gate, head held high, while Stevie scrabbled desperately for a foothold, hanging on to the saddle for dear life.

Carole, meanwhile, was doubled up with laughter. Lisa was giggling too as she finally got Belle into focus and started shooting. She got several good shots of Stevie's precarious ride before the mare moved out of range.

As Belle reached the fence, Stevie finally lost her grip for good and slid off the saddle, landing on the ground with a thump. She got up and dusted off her jeans, sheepish but unhurt.

"Nice technique, Stevie," a voice said dryly from just outside the ring. "Maybe I'll let you lead Tuesday's class, and you can give us all a refresher lesson on how to fall."

Stevie looked up and blushed. Max Regnery, her riding instructor and the owner of Pine Hollow, was leaning casually on the fence watching her, a bemused expression on his face. Beside him were Deborah Hale, his fiancée, and Judy Barker, a local vet.

"Oh, hi, Max," Stevie said. "I didn't see you there."

Lisa and Carole, leading their horses, joined Stevie by the gate and greeted the three adults. Lisa even snapped a quick picture of them.

4

"What are you doing here, Judy?" Carole asked, a little concerned. As far as she knew, the vet wasn't scheduled to visit any of the horses for checkups that day. "Is anyone sick?"

"No, nothing like that," Judy replied. "I'm here to be interviewed by our own roving reporter." She gestured to Deborah.

"That's right," Deborah said. She held up the pencil and pad of paper she was holding, showing the girls the pages of scribbled notes she'd already made. "I needed to pick someone's brain about horses, and Judy kindly volunteered."

Deborah was a newspaper reporter for the *Washington Times*. She and Max had met when she had been working on a story at the local racetrack and she had needed to learn about horses. They had become engaged a short time later and were planning to be married soon.

Carole looked surprised. "Well, Judy knows practically everything about horses," she said. When she had time, Carole liked to volunteer as Judy's assistant. She had learned a lot from working with the vet. "But why not just ask Max?"

Deborah glanced at Max and chuckled. "Well, Max knows practically everything about horses too," she said. "And I have been asking him dozens of questions, believe me—"

"Hundreds," Max interrupted with a smile.

"Thousands," Deborah admitted. "But the kind of

horses I need to know about for the article I'm writing are a little outside Max's realm of expertise. You see, I'm doing another racetrack article. A big one."

"Really?" said Carole, instantly all ears. Some time ago she had spent some time at the racetrack with Judy. She had even ridden in the post parade—when the horses parade in front of the stands before the race—leading Prancer, the horse Lisa rode. Prancer lived at Pine Hollow now because she'd been injured in that race and retired from the track. Her injury—caused by a weak pedal bone—kept her from being a good racehorse, but it didn't stop her from being a wonderful saddle horse, so Max and Judy had bought her for Pine Hollow.

Max nodded. "I'm surprised you girls can't guess what Deborah's story is about," he said teasingly, reaching out to scratch Belle behind the ears. "I thought you three knew everything there was to know about everything that has to do with horses. Did you happen to watch the Kentucky Derby last Saturday?"

The girls traded glances, then shook their heads. They all knew about the Kentucky Derby, of course. It was the most famous event in American Thoroughbred racing, when the top three-year-olds competed for a garland of roses—and a lot of prize money. But none of them had seen the race on TV that year.

"As I recall, that was the day you made us stay for hours measuring feed," Stevie told Max pointedly.

He just grinned in response to that. "Anyway," he

continued, "our Deborah here"—he put an arm around her proudly—"landed the plum job of covering the hot rivalry between the Derby winner and the horse that ran second."

"That's right," Judy said. "I'm sure you girls remember Mr. McLeod, right?"

"Of course," The Saddle Club answered in one voice. David McLeod was the owner of Maskee Farms, a Thoroughbred racing stable located near the girls' hometown of Willow Creek, Virginia. Judy was the vet who took care of his horses. Mr. McLeod had been Prancer's owner before the accident that had ended her racing career.

"Well, did you know that one of his horses ran second in the Kentucky Derby?" Judy asked.

Stevie, Carole, and Lisa gasped. "No way!" Stevie exclaimed.

"Way," Max replied tartly. "In fact, Mr. McLeod's colt came awfully close to winning. People are saying he might take the Preakness."

"That's the second race of the Triple Crown, right?" Carole said. Carole liked to know as much as possible about everything having to do with horses. She didn't know as much about Thoroughbred racing as she did about some other things, like show jumping or dressage, but she'd done some reading on it the last time she'd gone to the track. She knew the names of the three races that made up the Triple Crown—the Kentucky Derby, run at Churchill Downs in Kentucky; the Preakness, which took place at Pimlico racetrack in Baltimore, Maryland; and the Belmont Stakes, held at Belmont Park in New York. All three races were open only to three-year-olds, and all three were very prestigious and competitive. In the entire history of the races, only a few horses had managed to win all three.

"Right," Judy replied in answer to Carole's question. "It's being run next Saturday."

"And I'm going to be there to cover it," Deborah said. The Saddle Club thought she sounded a little nervous.

"Don't worry, Deborah," Judy reassured her. "You'll do well."

"I hope so," Deborah replied with a sigh. "It's nice to know I have you and Max rooting for me."

"And us," Stevie added, speaking for her friends. "We're your biggest fans."

Deborah smiled at them. "Thanks. I appreciate that," she said. "But there are one or two people who don't think so highly of me."

"Who?" Lisa asked.

"Well, since I'm fairly new at this racing game, a couple of the more experienced track reporters have been giving me a hard time," Deborah said. "There's one in particular who won't get off my case for a second. His name is Kent Calhoun, and he writes for the *Racing Times*. He's been around the track for his whole career, so he thinks I can't possibly know what I'm doing."

"That's ridiculous," Carole replied. "You've learned

8

more about horses since you met Max than any other six people possibly could."

"Well, that may be true," Deborah said. "But just because I've learned a lot about horses doesn't mean I know a lot about racing. There's a whole encyclopedia of information beyond just the horses—training, handicapping, statistics, history, you name it."

"No wonder you're looking for help," Stevie commented. She could sympathize. What Deborah was talking about sounded an awful lot like schoolwork to her—especially the history part.

Deborah smiled. "Right. If there are two things I've learned as a journalist, it's to do my research and to go on instinct. My instinct tells me I can do this story—so here I am, researching away." She glanced at Judy. "And it doesn't hurt that my own personal walking library happens to be the vet of one of my story subjects."

"What's Mr. McLeod's horse's name?" Lisa asked.

"Monkeyshines," Deborah replied. "He's a big, dark bay colt, very spirited. You girls would love him. He's got almost as much personality as Belle here." She laughed and pushed away the mare's head. Belle had been trying to nibble on Deborah's pencil.

"What's the other horse like?" Carole asked. "The one who won the Kentucky Derby."

"He's a great horse," Max said. "His name is Garamond. He's owned by Kennemere Farm in Kentucky."

"So he had the home court advantage," Stevie put in.

Inbred

"Well, sort of," Max said. "But several of the other Derby entrants were Kentucky-bred as well. No, Garamond has more than geography going for him. He's descended from Secretariat on his sire's side, and his dam is distantly related to Bold Ruler."

Stevie and Lisa looked mystified, but Carole nodded. In her reading she had encountered the names of both horses and knew that they were among the all-time stars of Thoroughbred racing history. She also knew that racehorses' bloodlines were important, since they were bred for just one thing—speed.

"Wow," Carole said. "Mr. McLeod's horse must be pretty spectacular if he can compete with a horse like that."

"He certainly is," Judy answered. "It's too bad you haven't been out to Maskee Farms with me lately, Carole. It's a rare thing to encounter a horse like that. David McLeod has been quite successful in racing for a while, but Monkeyshines is definitely his biggest star so far."

"Wow," Carole said again. "I guess the Preakness is going to be a great race."

"That's right," Max put in with a smile. "You girls will have to be sure to watch it on TV." He paused. "Well, on second thought, you may not have time. I was planning to ask you to help my mother look after things here next weekend while I'm away. I'm going to the race with Deborah, of course—did I mention that? Anyway, I was hoping you could help out—you know, muck out stalls, measure feed, things like that."

Stevie rolled her eyes.

Lisa was a little more polite. "Uh, sure, Max," she said. "We'll do anything we can to help."

Max nodded. "That's the spirit! I'll be sure to think of you while I'm at the track, watching all those big-name horses and jockeys, rubbing elbows with exciting and interesting trainers and owners, cheering the horses on—"

"Yeah, great," Stevie interrupted him. She couldn't believe the way Max was bragging. It wasn't like him, and it was getting on her nerves. She didn't really want to hear about the great time he would be having at the Preakness while The Saddle Club was toiling away at Pine Hollow.

Max seemed to get the hint. He smiled at the girls again and then turned to Deborah. "Come on, if you want to make it over to Maskee Farms today, we'd better get moving," he said.

Deborah nodded. "You're right." She glanced at Judy. "Do you want a ride over there?"

"How about if I give you two a ride?" Judy suggested. "I promised David McLeod I'd check on Hold Fast's hoof to make sure that infection is completely cleared up. I can drop you back here afterward on my way home."

"Sounds good," Max agreed.

"Hold Fast?" Carole put in. "Isn't that the stallion Mr. McLeod was planning to sell the last time I was there?"

11

"That's the one," Judy said. "He changed his mind about selling. Hold Fast was doing so well at the track that Mr. McLeod decided he'd make more money keeping him. In fact, he's running in a race on Preakness day."

Carole nodded. She had liked Mr. McLeod very much when she met him, but she also remembered how concerned he was with making money. It had made her realize that racing was a business, and she wasn't sure she liked that. She liked to think of riding as something to be done for fun, not for profit.

"Ready to go?" Judy asked Max and Deborah.

"Just about," Max said. "You two go ahead, and I'll meet you at the truck in a minute. I just have to tell my mother something first." Max's mother, known to all the riders as Mrs. Reg, helped run Pine Hollow.

As the three adults left, Stevie leaned on Belle's saddle and frowned. "It doesn't seem fair that Max gets to have a great time going to the Preakness while we get stuck here doing all his chores," she commented grumpily.

But Carole and Lisa weren't really listening. They were too excited at the thought that someone they knew had a horse competing in the Triple Crown.

"I hope Monkeyshines wins," Lisa said, slinging her camera over her neck and opening the gate.

"Me too," Carole agreed, heading through the gate with Starlight. "Although it would also be exciting if Garamond won all three races."

12

"Let's all get together at one of our houses and watch the race on TV next week," Lisa suggested. "I'm sure we'll be finished here in plenty of time, no matter what Max says."

"We can do it at my house if you want," Carole said. "My dad has to be at the base all day Saturday, so we'll have the place to ourselves. We can make popcorn and stuff and have a little party."

"Sounds great," Lisa said. She shook her head. "Just think how exciting it would be to see such a big race in person. Max is lucky."

"Exactly what I was thinking," Stevie put in. "And if you ask me, next Saturday should be our lucky day too."

"What do you mean?" Carole asked.

Stevie gave her friends a mysterious smile. "The Preakness is held in Baltimore, right?"

"Right," Carole confirmed.

"So why shouldn't we get to go too?" Stevie said. "I mean, Baltimore is practically right in our backyard."

"Well, not quite," Lisa said. "But it is pretty close."

"But you're forgetting one thing here, Stevie," Carole reminded her. "None of us can drive, remember? How are you planning to get there—on horseback?"

Stevie rolled her eyes. "Very funny. I was thinking that one of our parents could drive us, of course."

Carole was already shaking her head. "I just told you. My dad has to work all day next Saturday." Carole's father was a colonel in the United States Marine Corps. Her mother had died when Carole was eleven.

Stevie turned to Lisa. "How about your parents?"

"No good," Lisa said. "My aunt Maude is coming to town, and they promised to take her down to Colonial Williamsburg. They're leaving on Friday night—that's why I'm spending the night at your house, remember?" The girls had already planned a sleepover at the Lakes' house on the following Friday.

"How about your parents, Stevie?" Carole said. "Your dad was the one who took you and Lisa to the track last time."

Stevie looked glum. "No luck there," she admitted. "Both my parents are going to a wedding on Saturday afternoon." She threw up her hands in frustration. "There's got to be a way to get there," she cried. "Otherwise we're going to be stuck here mucking out stalls while Max and the others are off having the time of their lives at the Preakness. It's not fair. We've got to think of a plan."

The girls were still thinking furiously a few minutes later as they carried their saddles into the tack room. As they started soaping them, Mrs. Reg stuck her head out of her office. "Ah, there you are, girls," she said. "When you're finished with that, I wonder if you could help me out for a few minutes. There are some stalls that need mucking out, and Red just hasn't been able to get to them."

14

The Saddle Club exchanged glances. "Sure, Mrs. Reg," they answered in one voice.

When Mrs. Reg disappeared back into her office, Stevie added in a whisper, "We might as well get used to it."

As LISA TRUDGED home an hour later, her back aching as a result of her hard work with a pitchfork, she was thinking about what Stevie had said. But she wasn't feeling very optimistic about the chances of The Saddle Club's seeing the Preakness in person. They had no one to drive them and no money to pay for train tickets. Besides, Lisa wasn't sure her parents would let her go without adult supervision even if she had a way to get there.

When she arrived at her house, she went straight into the dining room, where her mother was setting the table. "Oh, there you are, dear," Mrs. Atwood said. "Hurry up and get changed. Dinner's almost ready, and your father and I have something important to discuss with you."

"What is it?" Lisa asked, setting her camera carefully on the sideboard.

"Just go ahead and change first," Mrs. Atwood said. "We'll have plenty of time to talk at dinner."

Feeling puzzled, Lisa did as she was told. It wasn't like her mother to be so mysterious. Mrs. Atwood hadn't seemed angry or upset, so that meant the news had to be something good. But what? When Lisa came back downstairs a few minutes later, both her parents were seated at the table waiting for her. "What did you want to talk to me about?" Lisa asked as she took her seat.

Her mother and father glanced at each other. Then Mr. Atwood spoke. "We just had an interesting phone call. . . ."

MEANWHILE, AT THE Hansons' house, Carole had just come downstairs after a quick shower and found her father in the kitchen chopping carrots for a salad. She joined him at the counter and began shredding a head of lettuce into a large bowl.

"Thanks, sweetheart," Colonel Hanson said. "You're always such a help in the kitchen. I probably don't tell you that often enough, do I? But it's true."

"That's all right, Dad," Carole replied with a shrug. "I like to help." She grinned. "Besides, the sooner this is done, the sooner we can eat. And I'm starved."

"Still, though, I can't help thinking that, as a good marine, I should remember the reward-and-punishment system we have in the Corps. It's always seemed to work pretty well in my experience—especially the reward part.

And I can't help thinking that sometimes a person deserves a reward just for being herself—oh, and for helping around the kitchen and that sort of thing, of course."

"What are you talking about?" Carole asked, heading for the refrigerator to get out the salad dressing. "Are you planning to give me a reward or something?" She turned from the refrigerator to see her father grinning at her.

"You might say that," Colonel Hanson replied.

"YOU MEAN I'M going to the Preakness?" Stevie was shrieking at that very moment.

"Ow, you just punctured my eardrums with your squealing," complained Stevie's older brother, Chad.

But Stevie wasn't paying any attention to him. "What did Judy say?" she asked her parents excitedly.

"Well, if you'd give us a chance to explain, we'll tell you the whole story," Mrs. Lake said, smiling at her excited daughter. "It seems that that stable owner, Mr. McLeod, has rented Judy a suite for the weekend at a hotel in Baltimore. Since her husband isn't going, poor Judy was afraid she'd be lonely. So she invited you girls along to keep her company."

"And Carole's dad and Lisa's parents are letting them go too?" Stevie asked.

Mrs. Lake nodded. "They are. We were the last ones Judy called. Everything's all settled."

"Hah! This will show old Max a thing or two," Stevie

couldn't help gloating. "He thinks he's so great just because he gets to go. Wait until he hears about this!"

Mr. and Mrs. Lake traded a glance. Mr. Lake cleared his throat. "Er, Stevie—I don't know how to break this to you, but apparently this whole plan was Max's idea. He even asked his mother to keep you girls at the stable for a few extra minutes today so he and Judy would have a chance to contact us and get everything settled before you girls got home."

Stevie's eyes widened. "Really? That—that rat!" she sputtered. "The way he pretended he was off to have this great time while we were stuck here, slaving away the whole weekend!" She broke into a wide grin. "I have to hand it to him. He was brilliant!"

The rest of the family exchanged amused glances. Coming from Stevie, a renowned schemer, that was high praise indeed.

She jumped out of her chair. "Hey, where are you going?" Stevie's twin brother, Alex, asked with his mouth full of peas.

"I've got to call Judy and thank her," Stevie explained, heading for the phone. "Then I have to call Carole and Lisa."

"Go ahead and call Judy if you want to, Stevie," Mrs. Lake said. "But I think Carole and Lisa can wait until after dinner."

"But, Mom—" Stevie began to say. But when she saw

the expression on her parents' faces, she decided not to argue.

AFTER DINNER STEVIE, Lisa, and Carole discussed the exciting news on a three-way phone call.

"It's going to be so great," Carole said dreamily. "It was exciting enough being at a small racetrack on a normal day. Just imagine, we'll be at one of the most important tracks in the country on one of the most important days of the year. Think of the fantastic Thoroughbreds we'll get to see!"

"I know," Lisa agreed. "I can't wait. It'll be a great chance for me to take some pictures of something new. I'm sure I can get lots of good action shots."

"Uh-huh," Stevie said, even though she had a feeling that photography was going to be the last thing on her mind the following Saturday. There would be so many more exciting things to think about. "How many races are there going to be before the Preakness?"

"I'm not sure," Carole said. "But I do know that Mr. McLeod has another horse running in one of the earlier races. It's Hold Fast—the stallion we were talking about earlier, remember?"

"Max will be able to tell us all about it on the way there," Stevie said. "I still can't believe the way he tricked us into thinking he was going and we weren't!"

"Didn't he do that to us once before?" Lisa said. "Remember the American Horse Show?" Once, without saying a thing to them about it beforehand, Max had called the girls' parents to ask if they could come to New York City with him for one of the most famous horse shows in the world. Their parents had said yes that time too.

"Well, I for one am willing to forgive him," Carole declared. "Especially since he volunteered to pick us all up on Friday and drive us to Baltimore. Boy, this sure beats staying home and mucking out stalls!"

Lisa and Stevie couldn't help agreeing with that.

"WHERE ARE THEY, where are they, where are they, where are they," Stevie muttered, peering up the empty road. She was standing in front of her school, Fenton Hall, on Friday afternoon. Classes had just ended for the week, and Max was due at any moment to pick up Stevie for the trip to Baltimore. But first he had to pick up Carole and Lisa at the public middle school on the other side of town.

Just when Stevie thought she couldn't possibly wait another second, she finally spotted Max's familiar station wagon coming up the road toward her.

"All aboard for Baltimore!" Max called out through the open window as he pulled the car to a stop in front of Stevie.

"Finally!" Stevie exclaimed as she climbed into the backseat beside Lisa and tossed her duffel bag over the seat behind her. "I thought you'd never get here."

"Well, we did get a little sidetracked . . ." Carole began to say.

"It's my fault," Lisa admitted.

Stevie noticed the large pile of camera equipment on the seat beside Lisa. Besides the camera itself, there were several lenses of varying sizes, a complicated-looking flash attachment, a small collapsible tripod, several other unrecognizable attachments, half a dozen rolls of film, a small spiral-bound notebook and pen, and a booklet called *Focus and You*.

"What's all that stuff for?" Stevie asked.

"I told you," Lisa replied. "This trip is the perfect chance to try out my camera in different kinds of situations. I just wanted to be prepared."

"That's why we had to stop at the drugstore so Lisa could buy four more rolls of film," Max said. "She was afraid she'd run out at a crucial moment."

"Hey, you never know," Lisa said with a smile. She began carefully repacking the equipment into her brown leather camera bag. When Lisa liked to do something, she liked to do it well, and she was willing to work hard at it. That was why she was a straight-A student, it was why she had become a good rider relatively quickly once she'd started, and it was why she was so eager to practice her photography now. And just as in riding, having the proper equipment was important to taking good pictures.

As Max drove out of town and merged onto the interstate, the girls settled back to enjoy the trip. Carole watched the trees flash by along the side of the road, thinking about Deborah's assignment. "Hey, Max," she said. "Do you think Deborah is really nervous about doing this story?"

"She has reason to be," Max replied. "It's a big story, and if she does well, it could mean a lot more racetrack assignments in the future. I think she'd really like that. But as she mentioned to you the other day, she's having some credibility problems with some of the established track reporters."

"Credibility?" Stevie repeated. "You mean they don't think she's a good enough reporter?"

Max shrugged. "How good a reporter she is doesn't really seem to matter to them. What matters is that she's relatively inexperienced with the racing world. And racing really is its own world in some ways. Some of the reporters—especially those who've been at the track for their whole careers—are probably pretty annoyed that someone new to it has been assigned a major story like the Triple Crown."

"That's terrible," Carole said. "They should at least give her a chance."

"Actually, most of them are doing just that," Max said. "They're not helping her any, but they're not getting in her way either. Although one or two of them—especially Kent Calhoun from the *Racing Times*—are doing their best to make her feel like an outsider."

"That's mean," Lisa commented.

23

"I agree," Max said. "It's too bad some people can't stand a little healthy competition."

"Speaking of competition," Carole said, "can you tell us a little about the race? I read about it when I was studying up on racing a while ago, but I don't really remember much."

"Sure," Max said. "First of all, the Preakness is the second of the three Triple Crown races."

"The Kentucky Derby is first and the Belmont Stakes is third, right?" Lisa volunteered. Carole had been lecturing her friends all week on everything she knew about racing, including that fact. She loved sharing her knowledge about horses almost as much as she loved acquiring it.

"Right," Max said. "The Preakness is the shortest of the three at a mile and an eighth, so it's important for the horses in it to be good sprinters. However, they also have to have serious stamina to run the longer distances in the Derby—a mile and a quarter—and the Belmont—a mile and a half, which is a really long distance for a horse to run at top speed."

"Why are these three races so important anyway?" Stevie asked.

"I guess it's mostly the history," Max said. "All three races have been run for well over one hundred years. The first Preakness, for example, was run in 1870."

"Wow!" Stevie said with a low whistle. "That *is* history!"

"And, of course, there's the money," Max continued.

"I *knew* it," Carole said. She still found the whole idea of horses as big business a little disconcerting.

Max chuckled. "I know it can seem like big business a lot of the time," he said. "But it's also a sport that a lot of people love for other reasons, and it has a long and noble history in this country and all over the world. That's why they call it the Sport of Kings."

"So how much money does the winner of the Preakness get?" Stevie asked.

"Well, I'm not sure exactly," Max admitted. "But I think it's several hundred thousand dollars. Plus there's a big bonus, something like a million dollars, for any horse that wins all three races in the Triple Crown."

The girls gasped. "No wonder people think these races are important," Lisa said.

Max nodded. "And besides the obvious and immediate value of the purse—that's what the money that goes to the winners is called—there's the added value that the horse gains by winning such a prestigious race."

"You mean a horse that wins even one Triple Crown race is worth a lot more money?" Carole asked.

"Right," Max confirmed. "And when that horse retires, his or her foals are automatically worth more."

Carole grinned at Max. "I don't know what Deborah needed Judy for," she said. "It sounds to me like you know an awful lot about racing!"

"I'm not quite as ignorant about it as Deborah may

have led you to believe," Max said with a smile. "But still, there's an awful lot to know, and Judy does know a lot more about most of it than I do. She worked at a racetrack full-time for a few years before setting up her practice in Willow Creek, so she knows more of the real ins and outs of racing."

"Well, it all sounds pretty complicated to me, especially the money part," Stevie said, leaning back and closing her eyes. "I just got out of math class, and I don't want to think about numbers anymore. Let's stop talking about money and get back to talking about the most important part of the race—the horses."

Laughing, the others agreed wholeheartedly.

LESS THAN TWO hours later, Max was pulling up in front of a high-rise hotel in downtown Baltimore.

"You girls wait in the car a minute while I go check on your room number," he said.

The Saddle Club waited impatiently for what seemed like hours. Finally Max reappeared, holding a card key.

"Okay, you're all set," he said. He handed the key to Lisa. "You've got only one of these for the three of you, so don't lose it."

"I won't," Lisa promised.

"Now, if you're interested, we could just drop your bags off in the room and head straight over to the track," Max said with a twinkle in his eye.

"If we're interested? You've got to be kidding," Stevie exclaimed. "Lead the way—and hurry!"

*   *   *

HALF AN HOUR later, The Saddle Club and Max entered the stable area at Pimlico racetrack, after a short stop at the gate to pick up the special passes Mr. McLeod had arranged for them. The passes would allow them free access to the stable area as well as the public areas of the track.

Carole looked around as they walked, trying to take everything in. There were busy people bustling about everywhere, just as there had been at the other racetrack, but everything seemed to be on a much larger scale. Everywhere she looked she saw something interesting. And everywhere she looked she saw tall, elegant Thoroughbreds, so beautiful they took her breath away. Carole loved all kinds of horses equally, but she had to admit that there was something very special about this aristocratic breed, the rulers of the racetrack.

"Come on, let's try to find Mr. McLeod's stable shed," Max said. He dug a wrinkled piece of paper out of his pocket and peered at it. "Deborah called last night with directions."

After a few false turns they found it. Judy Barker was outside the stable row, watching as a groom walked a handsome stallion in slow circles. Mr. McLeod was there too. The girls recognized him from their last trip to the racetrack.

"Hi, Max. Hi, girls," Judy called when she saw them.

"Hi!" Carole replied, gazing at the horse. "That's Hold Fast, isn't it?"

"You have a good memory," Judy replied with a smile. "I'm just doing one last check on his feet. I'm happy to say that they're completely healed. He's in good shape for race day tomorrow."

Mr. McLeod nodded hello to the girls and Max, but most of his attention was focused on Hold Fast. "You've finally convinced me, Judy," he told the vet. "He really does seem to be in perfect condition. Barring anything unforeseen, he'll race tomorrow." He nodded again to the group from Pine Hollow. "I'm glad you all could make it. Judy knows the layout around here pretty well, so I'm sure she'll show you around. But if you have any questions, just ask."

"Um, I have one," Lisa said shyly.

"Yes?" Mr. McLeod said.

"Could I take a picture of Hold Fast?"

Mr. McLeod laughed. "Of course you can!" he said. "You can take pictures of anything you want while you're here." He gestured to the groom, who turned Hold Fast to face Lisa.

Lisa raised her camera and fiddled with the lens. "Just a second," she mumbled. "I'm almost ready. . . ."

Mr. McLeod leaned over and removed the lens cap from Lisa's camera. "I think this might help," he said with a smile.

Lisa blushed as the others laughed. Then she laughed

29

too. "I guess I'm still kind of a beginner," she admitted. She quickly focused the camera and took the picture.

Mr. McLeod walked over and spoke to the groom, who led the stallion away. "Have fun," he told the girls and Max. "Judy, I'll see you later."

"What did he mean by what he said—that barring anything unforeseen, Hold Fast will race?" Carole asked as soon as Mr. McLeod was out of sight. "I thought he was already entered in a race tomorrow."

"He is," Judy replied. "He's been entered in the race for weeks now. Mr. McLeod had to pay an entry fee to qualify him. But he's been pretty worried about the hoof problem Hold Fast has been having lately. He was still considering scratching him—taking him out of the race —until today. But I think Hold Fast and I finally convinced him that everything's fine."

"Would Mr. McLeod have gotten his entry fee back if Hold Fast didn't race?" Stevie asked.

"I'm really not sure," Judy said. "I think he might have gotten part of it back, but not all of it."

"But he still would have kept him out of the race because Hold Fast might injure himself if he wasn't completely healthy, right?" Carole guessed. "Even if it meant losing money."

"Right," Judy said. "After all, if Hold Fast injured himself, Mr. McLeod would miss out on a lot more money, especially if Hold Fast couldn't race for a long time."

"Or forever," Lisa added, thinking of Prancer.

"Oh," Carole said. She hadn't been thinking of the money Mr. McLeod would lose if Hold Fast was injured. She had been thinking of Hold Fast. Judy's answer reminded her once again that the horses here at the track had to earn their keep by winning races.

"Hey, are we going to stand around here chatting forever, or are we going to meet the star?" Max interrupted.

"Okay, okay," Judy said with a smile. "Come on, I'll introduce you to Monkeyshines."

She led them into the stable and down the aisle, stopping in front of a large stall. A tall bay colt was peering out of it, his large, intelligent eyes watching the approaching group curiously. Both halves of the stall's door were open, and a nylon web was strung across the doorway at chest height to keep the horse inside. He let out a snort as they stopped in front of him.

"Is that him?" Carole whispered. "He's beautiful!"

"He sure is," Max said appreciatively. "Girls, take a good look. This is probably one of the most valuable horses you're ever going to meet in person."

"Look at his eyes!" Lisa exclaimed softly. "He's so sweet!"

Max rolled his eyes. But Judy chuckled. "He *is* sweet," she told the girls. "And he's very even-tempered. Racehorses aren't bred or trained to be friendly, but this one came by it naturally."

"Just like Prancer," Lisa said.

"Right," Judy said. "But unlike Prancer, this colt is all

business once he steps onto the track. He's got a real drive to win. When he's not racing, though, anyone would think he was some old coddled saddle mare—he loves people, and he's very gentle. You can pet him if you want."

Eagerly the girls reached forward to pat the colt's soft nose. Monkeyshines snuffled at each of them in turn.

"He's wonderful," Stevie said. "Lisa, you should definitely get a picture of this."

"Good idea," Lisa said. She raised her camera and peered through the viewfinder. But after fiddling with the lens for a moment, she lowered it again. "It's no good," she announced. "It's too dark here. And I left my flash attachment back at the hotel—I didn't think I'd be able to use it here. It might spook the horses."

"Don't worry," Max told her. "You'll have plenty of photo opportunities tomorrow. . . . Hey!" Suddenly he jumped forward, looking startled.

"What is it, Max?" Carole asked.

But Judy was laughing. "I know," she said. "Look."

The girls looked where she was pointing. There behind Max, gazing up at them and chewing thoughtfully on Max's sunglasses, was a small white goat with brown spots.

"That's Blackie," Judy explained, reaching down and gently prying the glasses away from the goat. "He's Monkeyshines's best friend."

"Really?" Lisa said dubiously. "A goat?" She had heard

of horses becoming attached to individual animals—cats, dogs, even chickens. But she had never met one who had adopted a goat.

"Sure," Judy said. "It's really not that uncommon. The great racer Seabiscuit had a goat as a companion. Some horses pick even stranger creatures—for instance, War Admiral, a very famous racehorse from the 1930s, had a pet rabbit. It traveled everywhere with him, and even followed him into retirement. These companion animals keep the horses happy—and if the horses are happy, they're likely to run better."

That made sense to all of them. The girls watched as Blackie strolled over to the tall Thoroughbred and looked up. Monkeyshines lowered his head and touched noses with the little goat, then let out a soft whinny.

"Hey! Did you hear that?" Stevie said. "It sounded like he just said hello!"

"Don't get carried away, Stevie," Max said. "You know horses don't understand English, and they certainly can't speak it."

"True, Max, true," Judy said with a grin. "But I think I may have to side with Stevie on this one. That sounded like a hello to me too." She turned to the girls. "That's why they always leave Monkeyshines's door open like that, with just the webbing across it. They want to make sure Blackie can get in and out of the stall."

"That's really neat," Lisa said. "I have just one question."

"What's that?"

"Why is he named Blackie?" Lisa asked logically. "There's not a speck of black on him."

Judy laughed. "Good question," she said. "Actually, Blackie is a nickname. His full name is Black Hole." She gestured to the goat, who had wandered over and started nibbling on a corner of Lisa's camera bag. "It's because everything disappears into his stomach. He'll eat anything and everything he can get his lips around. I lost a perfectly good ham and cheese sandwich to him yesterday when I set it down for half a second."

"I have to get a picture of him!" Lisa pulled her camera bag away from the goat and pointed the camera at him before she remembered the light problem. "Oh, rats. I guess it'll have to wait until tomorrow too," she said. She bent down and patted the little goat on the head. "Don't worry. I'll take a picture of you first thing tomorrow, I promise."

"Hey, Judy, who are all these strangers hanging around our goat?" a playful voice called out from behind them.

The girls turned to see a dark-haired young man approaching. He was wearing blue jeans and a T-shirt, and his face was stretched wide in a big grin.

"Hi, Eddie," Judy said. "Everyone, this is Eddie Hernandez. He's Monkeyshines's groom. Eddie, this is Lisa, Stevie, Carole, and Max—Deborah's fiancé."

Eddie nodded at the introductions. "I see you've already met my better half," he said, nodding toward the stall behind them.

"You mean Blackie?" Stevie joked.

Eddie laughed. "Very funny," he said. "I can see I'll have to keep an eye on you—Stevie, was it?"

"Nope," Stevie replied promptly. "My name is Carole."

"I think Eddie was referring to Monkeyshines—*Stevie*," Judy said pointedly. "Come on, girls. Let's get out of the way. I suspect Eddie has some work to do."

"Always," Eddie replied. "But that's okay. You don't have to leave. Blackie and Monk can entertain you."

"You call Monkeyshines Monk?" Lisa asked. "That's cute!"

Eddie laughed again. "I guess you could say that. It's also short. A lot of racers have nicknames. Makes things easier around the stable."

"That's right," Judy said. "Tell them Hold Fast's nickname."

"He's called Stretch," Eddie said. "That's because in his very first race, he came from behind in the homestretch—that's what we call the final straightaway before the finish line—and took home first-prize money."

"Wow," Stevie said. "That's wild."

"Well, most of the names aren't so interesting," Eddie admitted. He walked over to a mare in the next stall. "For instance, this is Ladyfingers. We call her Missy. And right next door to her is a gelding named Chestnut Cal. His stable name is Red."

Just then someone called for Eddie from farther down the shed row. "Whoops. That's the trainer," Eddie said. "Gotta go. But you'll be here for the big race tomorrow, right?"

"Definitely," the three girls said in one voice.

"Good," Eddie said with a grin. He gave Monkeyshines an affectionate pat. "You'll have fun watching old Monk walk away with it, then. He's a shoo-in to win, you know."

The three girls glanced at the tall colt, then grinned back at Eddie. "Definitely!" they all said again.

Carole watched Eddie hurry away. "I like him," she declared. "You can tell he really loves horses. Especially Monk."

"He's a good guy," Judy said. "Now, come on, I'll show you around the rest of this place."

"Great," Carole said. She'd been glancing curiously around the stable. At Mr. McLeod's stable, Maskee Farms, she'd been amazed at the spotlessness and order she'd seen. Now, even in this temporary home, the same sort of cleanliness and organization reigned. The path in front of the stalls was swept clean. The straw on the stall floors was fresh and new. There was a place for everything, and everything was in its place.

She mentioned this to Judy.

Judy laughed. "It's true," she agreed. "Mr. McLeod is

practically fanatical about that stuff, and it's a good thing. Like most horses, Thoroughbreds are delicate creatures despite their size and power. One loose nail lying around in their path or one stray bit of a food they're not used to can keep them off the track for days, weeks, even months. In the late 1970s a horse named Spectacular Bid had to be scratched from the Belmont after stepping on an open safety pin—and that was after he had already won the Derby and the Preakness. Mr. McLeod wants to do everything he can to avoid that kind of thing, so he's careful to take every precaution."

"Wow," Lisa said. "There seems to be so much to worry about with racehorses."

"That's for sure," Judy agreed, leading the girls down the shed row. "It's just like it is with any stable, except that in terms of money, the stakes are a lot higher."

"Speaking of high stakes, can we check out the competition now?" Stevie asked.

"You mean Garamond?" Judy said. "Sure thing. Right this way."

She led them out of the Maskee Farms stable shed and into the one next door. A young woman was sitting in a folding chair in the aisle near the entrance, reading a magazine. Behind her, a big bay colt with a gleaming mahogany coat stood quietly looking out over the half-door of his stall. The girls instantly guessed by his handsome head and regal bearing that this was the famous Garamond.

37

"Hello there," Judy greeted the other woman. "I'm Judy Barker, the vet for Maskee Farms. I'm showing these girls around and they asked to have a look at Garamond."

The young woman looked up and shrugged. "Be my guest," she said, gesturing lazily at the colt behind her. Then she seemed to remember her manners. "Oh, I'm Kelly Kennemere. My father owns Garamond."

Meanwhile, Stevie, Carole, and Lisa were gazing at the colt in awe.

"He's gorgeous," Carole breathed. "Can we pet him?"

"Better not," Kelly Kennemere replied dryly. "Not unless you want to lose a finger or two. He's not a pet, you know."

Carole frowned. She had just been asking; she knew very well that a lot of colts and stallions were unpredictable, especially with strangers. Kelly Kennemere didn't have to act as if the girls were kindergartners who had never seen a horse before.

Stevie wasn't impressed with Kelly Kennemere's attitude either, but she decided to try to be friendly. "Does Garamond have a stable name?" she asked. "If I worked here, I think I'd call him Prince. He looks so royal and proud and noble."

"I wouldn't know about that," Kelly replied with another shrug. "I'm just visiting from college. You'd have to ask one of the grooms." Even though the words were neutral, Carole once again thought she detected an unfriendly tone in the young woman's voice.

Meanwhile, Lisa was busy focusing her camera. "Hey, you guys," she said excitedly. "I think it's lighter in this stable. The 'insufficient light' signal isn't flashing. It must be because we're closer to the door." She carefully adjusted the lens. Finally she had the perfect shot in frame. She concentrated, checking the view for another second, then gently squeezed the button.

There was a whirring sound as she took the picture. But at the same precise second, Garamond suddenly tossed his head to dislodge a fly.

"Oh, rats!" Lisa cried.

"Tough luck," Carole said sympathetically. "Better try again." She turned to look at Garamond and noticed Kelly Kennemere smirking. "After all, it's not your fault the horse moved," she added loudly, feeling a little defensive of her friend.

Lisa nodded and peered through the viewfinder again. This time Garamond stood perfectly still while Lisa snapped his picture. "Great," Lisa said happily, replacing the lens cap.

"What's this, Kelly," came a loud, abrasive nasal voice from behind the girls. "You letting some kiddie-school paper scoop me or something?"

The Saddle Club turned to see a tall, lanky man approaching. He was wearing a rumpled suit and an insincere smile.

"Oh, hi, Kent," Kelly greeted him. "No, it's just some

tourists from Monkeyshines's stable who wanted to see what a winner looks like."

The man raised his eyebrows and looked over the Pine Hollow group. "I see. Well, I've got work to do here. I have an interview scheduled with Miss Kennemere. So if you wouldn't mind running along now, I can do my job."

Carole frowned. If she had thought Kelly Kennemere a little cold, it was nothing compared to the outright rudeness of this man. He seemed like a real jerk.

"Hey, listen here . . . ," Stevie began hotly, but Judy put a hand on her arm to stop her.

"It's all right," she said quietly. "We were just leaving."

As Judy led them away, Stevie turned to glare back at the rude man. "I can't believe that guy's nerve," she fumed. "Who does he think he is?"

Meanwhile, Lisa was putting two and two together. "Hey, Judy, is he by any chance the reporter who's been giving Deborah a hard time?"

"Bingo," Judy said grimly. "Kent Calhoun. He's a good enough reporter, but he sure can be unpleasant when he wants to be."

"You're not kidding," Stevie said. "He and that Kelly Kennemere are a perfect pair though. She was awfully unfriendly, wasn't she?"

By this time they had reached the Maskee Farms barn. "Where to next?" Carole asked, trying to put both Kent Calhoun and Kelly Kennemere out of her mind.

"Next, I think, is dinner," Judy replied. "I don't know

about you, but I'm starving. Let's find Max and see if he wants to join us for dinner and a mini-tour of Baltimore. As long as we're here, we might as well see the sights." She grinned. "I hope you all like seafood."

All three girls nodded. But Carole wasn't really thinking about dinner—she was thinking about everything she'd seen and heard that afternoon. Her last experience at the racetrack had taught her that some of the people there seemed to think more about the money that was at stake than about the horses themselves.

But now Carole was learning that there were all kinds of traditions and trivia that went along with racing. That meant it really was much more than just a business—didn't it?

As she followed her friends toward the parking lot, Carole decided she'd definitely be keeping her eyes and ears open the next day. She had a feeling she had a lot to learn.

4

"EVEN AFTER ALL that walking, I'm still so full I never want to eat again," Stevie moaned later that night.

The three girls were lying on the two large, comfortable beds in the second bedroom of Judy's spacious hotel suite. Judy had already said good night and gone to bed, but The Saddle Club was too excited by the day's events to go to sleep yet. They had decided to hold a Saddle Club meeting instead. Lisa was reloading her camera and getting her equipment ready for the next day while the girls talked.

"I know what you mean," Carole said. "I knew eating that last crab was a mistake, but it tasted so good, I couldn't resist."

Judy and Max had taken them to Baltimore's Inner Harbor, a modern complex of shops and restaurants by the water. The girls had been disappointed that they'd arrived too late to visit the famous aquarium there, but they had found plenty of other things to do, from shopping to people-watching to posing for dozens of Lisa's pictures. They had bought souvenirs for their families and stuffed themselves with fresh seafood until they could hardly move. And even after their huge meal, Stevie had insisted on ice cream for dessert—pistachio with coconut topping and strawberry sauce. Finally Judy had suggested heading back to the hotel to get some sleep.

"I can hardly wait for tomorrow," Stevie said.

"Me too," Lisa said, stifling a yawn. "And it's going to be here soon enough—it's almost midnight. What time did Judy say we'd be getting up?"

"I'm not sure," Carole said. "I just told her to wake us up in time to go over with her in the morning when she checks the horses before their workouts. She said it would be early."

FOUR HOURS LATER Lisa felt a hand shaking her shoulder. She groaned and rolled over without opening her eyes.

The hand didn't go away. "Come on, Lisa," said a loud, cheerful voice. "Rise and shine!"

Lisa slowly opened one eye a crack and peered up into Judy's smiling face. "What time is it?" she croaked.

"It's five minutes to four," Judy replied.

"Five to *what?*" Lisa said in disbelief. "Did you say five to *four?* As in four o'clock in the morning?"

"You got it," Judy said, reaching over to poke Carole, who was snoring softly in the other half of the bed. "We're running a little late, so you'd better hurry."

"Leave me alone, Dad," Carole mumbled sleepily. "It's Saturday."

Lisa, by now at least half awake, nudged Carole with her elbow. "Hey, wake up," she said. "We have to get over to the racetrack."

"The racetrack!" Carole said, suddenly wide awake. She sat up and rubbed her eyes. "Let's go!" She glanced down at her watch and gasped. "Is it really four A.M.?"

Judy was heading for the door. "I've got to finish drying my hair. I'll leave it to you two to get Stevie up."

Within forty minutes all three girls were dressed, though still yawning and rubbing their eyes. Judy led them out of the room and downstairs to the parking lot.

"I still can't believe I'm awake at this hour," Lisa groaned as she climbed into the backseat of Judy's car, clutching her camera.

Stevie slumped down in a corner of the front seat and fought to keep her eyes open. "I know what you mean," she mumbled. "And I thought *school* started too early!"

A few minutes later they were at the track, heading for the Maskee Farms stables. Despite the early hour, the stable area was bustling with activity. The Saddle Club watched as Eddie saddled Monkeyshines with a little help from Blackie, who seemed determined to chew on the ends of the horse's reins. Then Mr. McLeod and his trainer led the colt out to the track for his final prerace workout.

"Come on," Eddie said, noticing the girls watching. "You want to see him work, don't you?"

"You bet," Stevie said.

Eddie led The Saddle Club to a spot along the outside rail. "You'll have a pretty good view from here," he said. He pointed to a group of three horses galloping around the far turn. "As soon as that bunch is finished, Monk will have his turn. Mr. McLeod wants him to work alone today."

"What's he going to be doing, exactly?" Lisa asked.

"Well, since it's race day, this is really more of a warmup than a real workout," Eddie explained. "Monk will just trot for a half-mile or so to loosen up, and then gallop for another half-mile. But he won't be going at his full racing speed. He's got to save that for this afternoon."

Stevie noticed that there were a lot of other people standing at the rail farther down the track, watching as the horses exercised. "Who are they?" she asked Eddie.

"Some of them are reporters, some are the owners or trainers of other horses," he said. "They like to time the horses' workouts so they can see what their horses might be up against."

Carole looked more carefully. "Hey, there's Deborah," she said. Just then Deborah noticed the girls and gave them a quick wave before returning her attention to the horses on the track.

"She looks pretty busy," Lisa commented. She noticed that Kent Calhoun was also among the group, and wrinkled her nose, remembering his rudeness the day before.

A moment later she forgot all about Kent as the group of horses on the track finished their workout and left. It was Monkeyshines's turn. The jockey had arrived and mounted, and he was steering the eager colt onto the track. Lisa got her camera ready. She wanted to get plenty of pictures now in case she couldn't get close enough during the race.

If the girls had thought Monkeyshines was beautiful in his stall, they were even more impressed by seeing him in motion. Every move he made was smooth and controlled. Taut muscles rippled beneath his sleek coat as he trotted, then moved easily into a gallop.

"Wow," Carole said admiringly as Monkeyshines finished his workout and Eddie led the colt back toward the barn. "He's so perfect. He really is going to be hard to beat today, isn't he?"

"Hey, look," Stevie said. "Here comes his rival."

The others turned to see Garamond stepping calmly onto the track, accompanied by two other Thoroughbreds.

"Let's stay and watch him," Carole suggested.

"Good idea," Stevie agreed. "It couldn't hurt to see the competition in action."

The girls continued to lean on the rail as the big colt

and his two companions headed down the track at a walk. When they were halfway around, the riders turned the horses and began to trot, then canter. Finally, the three racers moved into a gallop.

Carole held her breath as the horses raced. Monkeyshines had seemed fast when running alone, but Garamond was equally impressive running in company. He quickly outdistanced his two rivals and swept over the finish line well in the lead. When his rider pulled him up, Carole could see that the big colt was hardly winded, and she guessed that he hadn't been running at his full speed. She couldn't hear what Garamond's trainer said to the jockey as he clipped a lead rope onto the colt's bridle, but he was smiling.

"He's going to be hard to beat too," she said.

Her friends nodded.

"But Monk can do it," Stevie said confidently. "After all, with The Saddle Club on his side, how can he lose?"

Carole and Lisa couldn't argue with that. They turned around and noticed Mr. McLeod and his trainer approaching the track, leading the gelding Chestnut Cal and another horse. The girls waved to them, then strolled off through the stable area, watching the hustle and bustle that was still going on all around them. When they reached the Maskee Farms stable, though, it was quiet.

"I guess the whole gang is at the track, watching the other horses," Carole commented.

It seemed to be true—there were no people in sight. In fact, the first creature the girls encountered, just outside the entrance, was Blackie the goat. He wandered over to them, chewing busily on a rag he'd obviously stolen from someone's grooming bucket.

"Oh, Blackie!" Lisa cried. "I promised I'd take your picture, didn't I?" She removed the lens cap from her camera and started to focus.

Carole and Stevie let out loud mock sighs. "Well, there goes the rest of the morning," Stevie commented jokingly.

"Very funny," Lisa said. "Just hold on a second. I've almost got him in focus." She moved forward a few steps, stumbling over a small rock that had somehow made its way onto the otherwise clean path.

Carole hurried forward and picked up the rock, tossing it into a nearby trash bin. "I wouldn't want that to get stuck in someone's hoof," she said.

"Like mine?" Lisa teased.

"Oh, come on," Stevie teased back. "If you're going to be an ace photographer, you're going to have to deal with bigger hardships than that little stone."

"True," Carole agreed, with a grin. "Like getting your subjects in focus before they fall asleep."

Carole and Stevie continued to trade jokes about Lisa's photography habit for a few moments while Lisa tried hard to ignore them and concentrate on getting the fast-moving little goat into focus.

"There!" she cried at last with satisfaction. "That was it! The perfect shot!"

"Finally," Stevie said. "Now can we go inside and say hello to Monk?"

The Saddle Club hurried through the open doorway and made their way toward Monkeyshines's stall at the end of the row. Halfway there, they noticed Hold Fast peering out at them over the half-door of his stall.

"Oh, hi there, Stretch!" Carole said, remembering the stallion's stable name. She paused to watch him for a few minutes, and her friends stopped with her. Blackie wandered away.

"He looks ready to race too, doesn't he?" Stevie commented. "Don't worry, Stretch, we won't forget about you just because you're not in the Preakness. We'll still cheer you on."

The Saddle Club turned and started toward Monkeyshines's stall again. But before they'd taken more than a few steps, they saw Blackie trotting toward them from the end of the row.

"Look, he found something else to chew on," Lisa commented. "It looks like hay. He must have snitched some from Monk."

Carole watched the goat for a moment. "It doesn't look like he's really eating it though, does it?" she said. "Maybe that rag filled him up."

Blackie shook his head, seeming annoyed. He spat out

the mouthful of hay. Then he picked it up again and worried it with his teeth. After a few seconds he spat it out again.

"What's this? Have pigs learned to fly?" said Eddie Hernandez's voice from behind the girls. "Did I really just see that bottomless pit spit out some food?"

Carole turned and saw that Eddie had an armload of hay and a couple of halters slung over one shoulder. His eyes were riveted to Blackie. "I guess he's full," she said with a shrug.

"Full?" Eddie shook his head. "I doubt it. We'd better ask your pal Judy Barker to take a look at him when she gets back. If Blackie has stopped eating, there's got to be something seriously wrong with him. Maybe I'll take a look at him myself when I have a half a second to do it." With that, Eddie disappeared into a nearby stall.

Carole was pretty sure the groom was joking, but just in case, she hurried forward and knelt down in front of the goat. "Are you feeling all right, Blackie?" she asked, scratching his head between the hard little horns. On a hunch, she leaned over and picked up the slightly soggy mouthful of hay the goat had dropped. She examined it for a second, then jumped to her feet. "Hey, you guys! Look at this," she exclaimed. "This hay is moldy through and through!"

Stevie and Lisa hurried over to see for themselves. "You're right," Stevie said with a low whistle. "No wonder Blackie didn't want to eat this. It would have made him as sick as—"

"Monkeyshines!" Carole interrupted her. She rushed off down the aisle. "If Blackie stole it from Monk's stall, there might be more. We have to get it before he does—if we're not already too late!"

"Oh, GOSH, SHE'S right," Lisa said, hurrying after Carole. Stevie was close behind her. All three of them knew that just a few bites of the moldy hay could make Monkeyshines much too sick to race that day.

Eddie reemerged from the other stall in time to see them racing down the aisle. "Whoa there, what's going on?" he shouted, hurrying after them.

Carole didn't pause to answer. Calling a greeting to Monkeyshines so he wouldn't be startled by her abrupt arrival, she quickly unlatched the webbing that was stretched across the open doorway and let herself in. She breathed a sigh of relief when she saw that the colt was facing away from his metal food manger. He greeted her with a nicker, and she reached out to pat him with her left hand, while her right hand searched the manger for more hay.

"Got it," she said a moment later, emerging from the stall and latching the rope carefully behind her. She was clutching a handful of moldy hay.

Eddie reached them at the same moment. "All right, what's going on here?" he demanded, sounding a little angry. "Don't you know you shouldn't go barging into a racehorse's stall like that, no matter how good-natured he is?"

"Sorry," Carole said. "I do know. But this was an emergency." She held out her hand so the groom could see the hay. "I had to stop him from eating this."

Eddie took the hay from her and examined it. The angry lines in his face relaxed, and he looked puzzled. "Moldy hay. How did you know this was in there?"

"That's what Blackie had that he wasn't eating," Stevie explained. "Carole saw that it was moldy, and she figured it must have come from Monk's stall. She didn't want him to eat it and get sick."

Eddie's eyes widened. He looked down in time to see Blackie scoot under the rope and into Monkeyshines's stall. "Boy, it's a good thing that goat is such a pig!" he exclaimed. "That was good thinking on your part, Carole —I can't believe I didn't think to stop and check on Blackie myself. I should know better than to just let that kind of strange behavior go, no matter how busy I am."

He handed the moldy hay back to Carole and quickly

stepped inside several of the other stalls nearby, checking the hay in each. "Nothing in any of these. Looks like Monk was the only unlucky one. It's a good thing you girls caught it in time. Otherwise Monk would have ended up out of the race with a bad case of colic." He shook each of the girls' hands in turn. "Thanks."

"You're welcome," said Carole. "Although Blackie probably deserves most of the credit. How do you think that moldy hay got in there anyway?"

Eddie shrugged. "Who knows? I fed the horses myself this morning and I know the hay was fine then. I also know that Monk polished off every bite of his breakfast—the trainer wouldn't let him run today if he hadn't. Someone must have given him some more hay later and not checked it carefully enough."

"That seems kind of strange . . . ," Lisa began to say slowly.

"Hey, stranger things have happened," Eddie said with another shrug. "It was a close call, but luckily it seems to have turned out okay. I'll ask Judy to give Monk a close look when she shows up, but other than that, all we can do now is forget about it."

"But—" Carole objected.

"Don't worry about it," Eddie said. "It was probably an accident." He hurried off down the aisle.

Carole, Stevie, and Lisa traded glances. They were silent for a moment.

"Do you think it was an accident?" Carole asked at last.

"No way," Stevie said. "How could moldy hay just accidentally end up in the feed bin of one horse—one horse who happens to be running in the Preakness that very day?"

"It does seem kind of suspicious," Carole agreed, staring down at the hay in her hand. "This isn't just a little moldy—it's moldy through and through. It would have been hard for someone to miss it." She shuddered as she thought about Monkeyshines's close call. If he'd eaten the hay and gotten colic, he would have been very sick—he might even have died. From all her experience of working with horses, Carole had learned that it was always better to be too cautious than not cautious enough. That meant always checking hay and other feed for spoilage. And right now that also meant wondering if there might be some other explanation for the moldy hay than "accident."

Lisa looked thoughtful. "I don't know, you guys," she said. "I agree that it's strange, but it must be an accident. What other explanation is there?"

"I'll tell you: Someone was trying to poison Monkeyshines," Stevie said darkly. "Someone knew that his owner and trainer and most of the other people from the stable were out with the other horses. Eddie was over getting hay, so he was out of the way. It was a perfect opportunity to knock Monk out of the race."

55

Carole stared at her friend. "But why?" she asked. "Why would someone do that?" She reached out and stroked Monkeyshines's nose. "What a horrible thing to try to do!"

Stevie nodded in agreement. "It is terrible," she said. "And we've got to find out who did it. This calls for a Saddle Club investigation! Lisa, why don't you get a few pictures of the scene of the crime?"

Lisa still looked unconvinced. "I don't know, Stevie," she said. "Why do you think it was a crime and not just a stupid mistake? Everyone around here is so busy today— maybe someone just didn't check the hay carefully enough, like Eddie said."

"Well, it's possible," Stevie said grudgingly. "But we should try to find out who it was so it doesn't happen again."

"I guess you're right," Lisa said uncertainly. She snapped on her flash attachment and quickly took a few photographs of Monkeyshines's stall and manger, though she wasn't sure what good it would do—there was obviously no evidence there now.

"Here, get a shot of this," Carole suggested, holding up the moldy hay she was still clutching.

Lisa obligingly focused on the hay and snapped a few pictures of it. Then the girls drifted back toward the stable entrance, discussing possible suspects.

"The first thing we need to figure out," Stevie said, "is a motive."

But before she could go any further with that line of thought, Max and Deborah entered and spotted them.

"There you are," Max called. "Judy thought we might find you here."

Deborah held up several white paper bags. "We brought breakfast."

"Breakfast," Carole repeated blankly. Her stomach grumbled. "Oh! What time is it?"

"It's after seven," Max said brightly. "We brought doughnuts and juice for all of you."

"Great!" Stevie said, taking one of the bags Deborah was holding and peering hungrily inside.

"Enjoy," Max said. "We've got to get going."

"Aren't you going to have breakfast too?" Lisa asked.

"We already ate," Deborah told her. "I've got a ton of work to do on my story before post time. Max is going to help me."

"That's right," Max said with a grin. "Deborah has been such a good sport about learning everything there is to know about *my* job and pitching in at Pine Hollow that I thought I'd return the favor. I'm now her official pack mule and gofer. So you girls are on your own for a while."

After Max and Deborah had left, The Saddle Club settled down in an empty stall to eat their breakfast and continue discussing the moldy hay incident.

"All right, first of all, let's come up with a list of likely suspects," Stevie said.

Lisa shook her head. "We can't do that until we figure out what anyone would gain by poisoning Monkeyshines."

"That's obvious," Carole said. "Someone must have wanted to keep him from racing today so that Garamond would win."

"That seems a little *too* obvious," Lisa pointed out. "I seriously doubt anyone from Garamond's stable would do something so risky."

"Don't be so sure," Stevie said, poking a straw into her juice box and taking a big gulp. "After all, everyone around here keeps talking about how much money is at stake. Who knows what someone would do for money?"

Lisa dug a notebook and pen out of her camera bag. "All right," she said. "I'm still not sure there's really a crime here to be solved, but just in case there is, we'd better look at this logically."

Carole and Stevie grinned at each other. Lisa could always be counted on to bring logic into any dilemma.

"Great," Stevie said. "First, write down all the possible motives someone could have."

Lisa nodded and wrote MOTIVES at the top of the page. Under that she wrote MONEY. Then she paused and stared at her friends. "Well?"

"How about revenge?" Stevie suggested.

"Revenge?" Carole said. "Where do you get that?"

"I don't know." Stevie shrugged. "That's always a motive in the movies. Maybe someone out there hates Mr.

McLeod passionately and wants to make sure his horse doesn't win."

Lisa looked more doubtful than ever, but she wrote REVENGE under MONEY. "I have another one," she said. She wrote ACCIDENT.

Stevie looked over her shoulder. "Accident?" she said.

"Yes. If we're going to investigate, we have to consider the possibility that there's no big conspiracy at all behind that moldy hay," Lisa said, looking a little stubborn.

Carole knew there was no point in arguing with Lisa when she had that expression. Besides, there was just the slightest chance she was right. "Okay, then," she said. "We have the motives. Now let's move on to suspects."

"Great," Stevie said quickly. "I nominate Kelly Kennemere."

Carole raised her eyebrows. "Good one!" she said approvingly. "She was really nasty to us yesterday. Maybe it was because she knew we were from Monkeyshines's barn and she had a guilty conscience."

Lisa wrote SUSPECTS and jotted Kelly's name underneath. "Who else?" she asked.

Stevie thought hard. "Well, there's Kelly's father," she said. "After all, he's the one who would profit the most if Monk were out of the race. Garamond would be almost certain to win the first-prize money."

"I guess so," Lisa said. "Although there's a chance he would anyway—he already won the Kentucky Derby, remember?"

"Write him down anyway," Carole said. "We don't know what kind of person Mr. Kennemere is. He could be super-greedy or just super-mean. Judging by his daughter, I wouldn't doubt it."

"I still don't think someone like that would take such a big risk," Lisa said as she wrote Mr. Kennemere's name under his daughter's. "Although I suppose it could have been someone else in his stable—maybe the jockey. Doesn't he get a percentage of whatever money the horse wins?"

"You're right," Carole said. "Write that down."

Lisa wrote THE JOCKEY OR SOMEONE ELSE IN THE STABLE.

The girls continued to think as they finished their breakfast, but they couldn't come up with any more likely suspects.

"Well, we've got three suspects on our list. The best thing to do," Stevie suggested as they stood up and walked to the nearest trash can to deposit their bags and cartons, "is to keep our eyes and ears open for the rest of the day. Maybe we'll see or hear something that will give us a clue."

"This reminds me of our last mystery-solving Saddle Club project," Carole said. "When we solved the horse-napping." The girls had once tracked down and rescued several valuable horses that had been stolen from Pine Hollow.

"Actually, this time we'll be just like Deborah when she's on an assignment," Lisa said. "We'll investigate every angle as if we were researching a newspaper story. It could be fun, even if we don't find out anything. I'll have my camera ready to record any suspicious characters."

"That is, if they're willing to stand still for half an hour while you get them in focus," Stevie teased.

Lisa arched her eyebrows. "You'll see. My camera could be the thing that cracks this case."

"One thing we should definitely do," said Carole, who had been thinking so hard she'd missed the whole exchange, "is keep a close eye on Monkeyshines for the rest of the day."

Stevie and Lisa sobered instantly.

"That's true," Stevie said. "When whoever did it finds out Monk didn't eat that hay, he or she might try again."

"Come on," Carole said. "Let's go check on him now."

As soon as they turned the corner into the corridor leading to Monkeyshines's stall, they saw that the big colt already had a visitor. A short, wiry man wearing a green baseball cap was standing in front of the stall, staring at the horse, who was looking out at him curiously. Blackie was peering out of the stall too, chewing thoughtfully on the handle of a curry comb.

Stevie, immediately suspicious, strode quickly down the aisle toward the stranger. "Hey, you there," she called. "What are you doing?"

The man looked startled for a second. Then his face twisted into a scowl. "Who's asking?" he replied shortly.

Stevie stopped in front of him, her hands on her hips.

Her friends stood behind her. "*I'm* asking," she replied loudly. "I'm a friend of Mr. McLeod's, and I want to know what you want with his horse. If you're not willing to tell me, maybe I should go get him."

"You're a friend of McLeod's, huh?" the little man said with a snarl. "Well, there's no law I know of that says I can't come into a stable and look at any horse I want—even if it *is* McLeod's precious Monkeyshines. And I don't think I have to explain anything to him *or* to you. How do you like that?" Without waiting for an answer, he shoved his way past the girls and hurried down the aisle toward the entrance. A moment later he was gone.

The three girls stared at one another.

"Wow," Carole said after a moment. "I think we just found suspect number four."

Stevie nodded. "Definitely," she said, gently pushing Blackie away from her shoelace, which he was trying to chew. "He acted like someone with something to hide. And he knew who Monkeyshines was, *and* Mr. McLeod."

"There's just one problem," Lisa pointed out. "We don't know who he is."

"Let's ask Eddie," Stevie said.

As if on cue, the groom stepped out of the spare stall that was being used as a tack room. He didn't notice the girls, however—he just walked quickly to the entrance and went out.

"Quick, we've got to catch him," Carole said, leading the way. When she emerged into the morning sunshine, she looked around and spotted Eddie striding away down the shed row, quickly glancing from left to right as he walked.

"There he is," Stevie said beside her. She opened her mouth to call Eddie's name, but Carole shushed her.

"Just a second," she said. "I may be crazy, but doesn't Eddie look as though he doesn't want to be noticed?"

Lisa shook her head. "You *are* crazy," she said. "Don't tell me you're so caught up in this conspiracy theory that you'd suspect even Eddie! He adores Monkeyshines—why would he want to hurt him?"

Meanwhile Stevie was staring intently after the groom. "I'm not so sure Carole is crazy after all," she said. "It does look like Eddie doesn't want anyone to see him, and I think I know why. Look where he's heading."

Carole gasped. "Garamond's stable!"

Stevie nodded grimly. "I think that means we have *two* new suspects to add to that list!"

A COUPLE OF hours later Lisa glanced at her watch. "It's only nine A.M.," she exclaimed. "I can't believe it! It feels as if a whole day has passed already."

"Time flies when you're having fun," Stevie said. The three girls were outside Mr. McLeod's stable, leaning against the wall and watching the activity surrounding them, which had slowed down only a little since earlier that morning.

"Being here is fun," Carole agreed. "The only part that's not so much fun is thinking that Eddie may have been the one who tried to poison Monk." After seeing the groom sneaking over to Garamond's stable, The Saddle Club had waited outside. Eddie had come out a short time later, glancing all around as he hurried back to his own stable. Reluctantly, the girls had added him to their list of suspects along with the rude, wiry little stranger who'd been standing in front of Monkeyshines's stall.

"If it was Eddie who did it, I hope he doesn't try again," Stevie said. "After all, he's Monk's groom. It would be easy for him."

"Not that easy," Lisa pointed out. "Now that all the horses have been exercised, Mr. McLeod and Judy and the trainer and jockeys and the other grooms and who knows who else will all be around the barn until race time. Eddie wouldn't dare try anything with all those people around."

"I guess not," Stevie admitted, kicking at the dirt with the toe of her sneaker.

"Well, I for one am still not convinced he did it," Carole said. "He just seems too nice. And he did seem truly surprised when we found the hay."

"Acting," Stevie said promptly. "Still, we should keep on investigating our other suspects. Especially the Kennemeres—whether they're working on their own or in cahoots with Eddie, we need to find out more about them."

"Agreed," Carole said. "But how?"

"Easy," Stevie said. "We spy on them."

"Spy?" Lisa echoed. "I'm not sure that's such a good idea."

"Come on, Lisa, don't be chicken," Stevie said. "You wanted a chance to be an investigative photojournalist, right? Well, this is it!"

Lisa glanced at Carole. "What do you think?"

Carole thought for a moment. "I don't know," she said at last. "It does seem a little risky. But on the other hand, we're doing it to find out who tried to hurt Monkey-shines. And I think that's the most important thing right now." That was a typical Carole response. She always put horses first and foremost in every decision.

Lisa rolled her eyes. "All right, I guess I'm outvoted. You guys win. Let's go play James Bond."

Ten minutes later The Saddle Club was hidden behind a stack of hay bales near the entryway of the Kennemere stables. By peeking around the corner of the bales, they had a view of the entrance as well as of Garamond's stall. The big horse had watched curiously as the three girls peeked into the shed, held a quick whispered conference, and tiptoed over to their hiding place. But he hadn't made a sound.

"It's awfully lucky that no one was around," Lisa whispered. "Otherwise our cover would have been blown right away when they saw us looking in."

"I just hope someone shows up soon," Stevie said worriedly. "Where are they all anyway? You'd think someone would be keeping an eye on Garamond."

Carole was peeking out at the doorway. "Shh!" she hissed. "Here comes someone. It's Kelly!"

"What's she doing?" Stevie whispered eagerly.

"Just a second—I'll tell you—okay, she's looking at Garamond," Carole reported in a low whisper. "Now she's turning around." She ducked back as far as she could to avoid being seen. "She's setting up that folding chair that was leaning against the wall. She's sitting down on it, and pulling something out of her pocket—oh, it's a paperback book. Now she's sitting and reading."

Carole moved back and crouched beside her friends. "There you have it. She's relaxing with a good book. Now what do we do?"

"I knew we shouldn't have done this," Lisa moaned. "We could be trapped here for hours while she reads."

"Don't give up yet," Stevie whispered. "Someone else could still come in and talk to her. Maybe Eddie will come back to go over their plot. Or maybe it'll be her father. We have to wait."

"No kidding," Lisa said dryly. "What choice do we have?"

Carole was looking up at the topmost of the bales before them. "Don't look now, but we have company," she said quietly.

Stevie and Lisa looked up too. There, perched on the edge of the bale, looking down at them, was a very large, very fat white chicken.

"What do you think she wants?" Stevie asked.

"I don't know." Carole stared at the chicken. "Nice birdie," she whispered tentatively.

As if in reply, the chicken let out a sudden loud squawk.

"What's wrong, Lulu?" Kelly Kennemere's voice asked

from the other side of the bales. The chicken squawked again and flapped its wings, still staring at The Saddle Club.

Lisa gulped. "Go away," she ordered the bird. "Get lost, Lulu."

But Lulu didn't get lost. Instead, with another mighty squawk she hurled herself downward, straight at the girls.

"Aaah!" Carole shrieked, holding up her hands to protect herself. Lulu landed on the ground beside her with a thump. Carole peeked at the bird through her fingers. Lulu calmly bent down and started pecking at some stray pieces of hay on the floor.

Meanwhile, quick footsteps could be heard approaching the bales. "All right, who's back there?" Kelly Kennemere demanded cautiously, her voice quavering a little. "Come out of there right now."

Feeling very sheepish, the three girls crawled out of their hiding place and stood up. Lulu followed, clucking softly.

When she saw who the intruders were, Kelly looked surprised. "Aren't you the girls from Maskee Farms?" she asked. "You came around here last night, right? What in the world were you doing back there?"

"Uh, that's right, we were here last night," Stevie said, thinking fast. "We were, um, so impressed with Garamond that we had to see him again."

Kelly looked skeptical. "His stall is over there, not back behind the hay."

68

"Right," Stevie said. "But Lisa, here, is a photographer, you know?" She thumped the startled Lisa on the back. "Right, Lisa?"

"Oh, uh, right," Lisa said. She held up her camera. "See?"

"So she wanted to get a few more pictures of Garamond," Stevie continued, gathering confidence now. "The light wasn't very good in here last night. There wasn't anyone around when we came in, but we thought it would all right if we just came and took a few quick pictures. Then when Lisa took off her lens cap, she dropped it and it rolled away behind those bales."

"And all three of you had to go back and get it," Kelly finished, still looking suspicious.

"Well, she couldn't find it at first," Stevie said lamely. "We were helping her."

"How long were you back there anyway?" Kelly demanded.

Stevie cocked an eyebrow at her. "Not long. Why do you ask?"

Kelly frowned at her. "No reason." She nodded at Garamond. "You can take a couple of pictures if you hurry. But then you'll have to leave. We don't want him to get overexcited with too many visitors before the race."

Stevie nudged Lisa in the ribs. "Oh, uh, okay," Lisa stammered, raising her camera. She removed the lens cap and began her usual fiddling.

"Just get the picture, will you, Lisa," Carole said, trying

to sound casual. She watched as Lulu the chicken strolled over to the stall next to Garamond's and flapped her way up onto the top of the half-door. A chestnut horse moved over to the door and snuffled at the bird.

Kelly noticed where Carole was looking. "Lulu is Miss Philippa's pet," she explained.

"Does Garamond have a pet?" Carole asked curiously, watching the chicken.

"No," Kelly said shortly.

Just then Lisa finally snapped Garamond's picture. "Got it," she announced, sounding relieved.

"All right, that's all," Kelly said. "You've got to leave. And it would be better if you didn't come around here again before the race." She shooed them toward the door.

The red-faced Saddle Club didn't have to be told twice. They scurried for the door.

Once safely outside, they stopped to catch their breath.

"Well, that was embarrassing," Lisa said, still blushing.

"Yeah, but did you see Kelly's face when she caught us?" Stevie exclaimed, her eyes bright. "She had guilt written all over her! She was obviously afraid that we'd seen or heard something incriminating."

Carole shrugged. "She did seem pretty nervous about something," she admitted. "I think we can consider it a clue. Write it down, Lisa."

Lisa flipped open the notebook and jotted down a few words. "It may be a clue, but it's far from being hard evidence," she said. "We can't accuse someone of horse poisoning just because she seems a little nervous."

"The more clues we get, the closer we are to finding the culprit," Stevie said wisely.

Lisa rolled her eyes. "All right, all right. Just promise me one thing."

"What's that?" Stevie asked.

"Promise me that if and when we do figure out this thing, you'll stop using words like 'culprit.'"

Stevie grinned. Usually Lisa, the A student, was the one who used fifty-cent words like "culprit." "It's a deal," she promised.

Suddenly Carole gasped. "Don't look now," she warned. "But here comes one of our suspects."

Her friends turned and saw the wiry little man they'd encountered earlier. He was walking quickly toward them, his hands shoved deep in the pockets of his jeans and his eyes trained on the ground in front of him. His face wore a deep frown beneath the rim of his baseball cap.

The girls shrank back against the stable wall behind them. "Quick, Lisa," Stevie whispered urgently. "Get his picture."

Lisa fumbled with her camera, trying to focus on the fast-moving man. Less than a dozen yards from the girls, his face was perfectly framed by the camera's viewfinder. "Got him!" Lisa whispered triumphantly. She pressed the button to take the picture. There was a soft click—and then a loud whirring sound. "Oh, rats," Lisa whispered. "It's the automatic rewind!" She stared helplessly at the camera as the noise continued.

The wiry man had heard the noise too, and looked up. "Hey," he said angrily. "Did you just take my picture?"

"Uh, no?" Lisa lied, her voice little more than a squeak. "I'm just rewinding my film, see?" She held up the camera.

The man glared at her balefully, then at Stevie and Carole. With an angry snort he turned and hurried away, muttering under his breath.

Lisa let out her own breath in a whoosh. "What a horrible man!" she exclaimed.

"Come on," Stevie said, grabbing her by the arm. "We've got to find out who he is!"

They hurried back to Mr. McLeod's stable shed. As they rushed inside, they almost collided with a short, slim man who was coming out. "Whoa! Where's the fire?" he asked with a laugh. He looked at Carole. "Hey, I know you—you're the girl who was out to steal my job a while back! Prancer's friend, right?"

Carole smiled back at him. "Right. Hi, Stephen," she said. "These are my friends Stevie and Lisa. This is Stephen, Mr. McLeod's jockey."

"Well, one of 'em, anyway," Stephen said cheerfully, reaching out to shake the girls' hands. "So how is that fine filly Prancer anyway?"

"You should ask Lisa about that," Carole told him. "She's the one who rides her most of the time."

"That's right," Lisa said, looking up from her camera. She had just removed the used roll of film and was popping in a new one. "And she's absolutely wonderful. I'm so glad Max and Judy were able to buy her for Pine Hollow."

"Well, I'm glad too," Stephen said. "She's a sweetheart of a horse, and she's probably a lot happier at a riding stable than she was at the track."

"Not like Monkeyshines though, right?" Carole said.

"No way," Stephen agreed. "That colt loves to race, and he loves to win. He came mighty close in the Derby, and I think today just might be his day."

"We do too," Stevie said. "We think he's sure to win."

"You're not the only ones," Stephen told her. "I just checked the morning line, and right now both Monk and Garamond are listed at almost even odds."

Carole giggled. "Even odds?" she repeated. "What does that mean?"

Stephen laughed. "I guess it does sound a little weird, doesn't it?" he admitted. "It just means that so many people are guessing the horse will win that his predicted odds are really close. For instance, Monk is listed at two to one. That means that if he wins, anyone who bets on him to win will make back two dollars for every one bet. Garamond is the favorite, so his odds are even lower—six to five."

73

"So people would get back six dollars for every five they bet?" Lisa guessed. "That's not much of a profit, is it?"

"Not really," Stephen said. "Especially when you consider that some of the other horses in the race are listed at ten to one, twenty to one, or higher. But the important thing is, Monk's and Garamond's odds just show how well both horses are regarded. Those odds will probably go even lower as the day goes on and more people place their bets."

Stevie was growing impatient with the conversation. "Listen, Stephen, we have a question about something. Maybe you can answer it," she began.

He shrugged. "I'll do my best. Fire away."

"We keep seeing this man around the track, and we were wondering who he is," Stevie explained. "He's about your height and weight, with dark hair and a mean look on his face. He was wearing an ugly green baseball cap and jeans."

Stephen laughed. "Green baseball cap? That'd be Duncan Gibbs. He's a jockey too. In fact, he used to ride for Mr. McLeod."

"Really?" Stevie said, shooting her friends a look. This sounded like a clue.

"Yep," Stephen said. "He was Monk's first jockey. They won two races together last year."

"What happened?" Carole asked.

Stephen's smile faded and he shook his head, looking

74

grim. "That was a bad situation. What happened was Monk's third race. It was a longer one than he'd run in before, and the trainer was a little worried that it might be too much for him. He told Duncan to hold Monk back for most of the race, and let him go only at the end."

"So Monk could conserve his strength?" Carole asked.

"Right," Stephen said. "That was before we knew what an all-around great racer Monk really is. But anyway, Duncan decided he knew better than the trainer how the race should be run—he took Monk straight to the lead and kept him there wire to wire."

"So he won?" Lisa said. "Then what was the problem?"

"The problem was Duncan deliberately went against the trainer's orders," Stephen explained. "There was no reason for that kind of performance. Monk could easily have won by running the race the way the trainer wanted. And worse, if he had had just a little less stamina, he might have been so badly tired that he could have injured himself, or dropped back and finished out of the money."

"So why did Duncan do it?" Carole asked.

"Nobody knows," Stephen said. "Personally, I think he might have been showing off for someone. He's not an easy guy to get along with—he's always trying to start feuds or rivalries with the other jockeys. In any case, the trick with Monk cost him his job with Mr. McLeod—and one of the best mounts of his career." He shook his head. "I think Mr. McLeod might have forgiven Duncan even after what he did if he had just apologized for it. But he wouldn't. And when Mr. McLeod did fire him, Duncan blew up and went a little crazy. He even threatened Mr. McLeod."

The Saddle Club exchanged wide-eyed glances.

"He threatened him?" Carole said. "What did he say exactly?"

Stephen shrugged. "I don't remember exactly. It doesn't really matter anyway—Duncan is just a blowhard. Deep down he's not a bad guy, really. He just needs to learn to control his temper."

At that moment one of the grooms poked his head around the corner and told Stephen that the trainer needed to see him.

"Well, I'll see you girls later," Stephen said, turning to follow the groom. "Don't forget to cheer for me and Monk in the big race."

"We won't," The Saddle Club promised in one voice.

As soon as Stephen was out of sight, Stevie turned to her friends. "See? My revenge theory wasn't so crazy after all," she said excitedly. "Duncan must be the one. I'm practically sure of it."

"But, Stevie," Carole protested, "you're also practically sure that Kelly Kennemere did it, *and* that Eddie did it. They can't all have done it."

"It had to be Duncan," Stevie said. "It makes perfect sense. After all, Stephen just said that Duncan threatened Mr. McLeod."

"He also just said that Duncan would never do anything about his threats," Lisa reminded her.

Stevie waved that argument aside. "I still think Duncan Gibbs belongs at the top of our suspect list," she declared.

"YOU KNOW," CAROLE commented a few minutes later, "we've been spending so much time trying to solve this mystery—"

"Or *possible* mystery," Lisa added.

"Okay, *possible* mystery," Carole said, "that we've hardly had time to check out the other horses who'll be running in the Preakness."

"True," Lisa said. "Let's go see a few of them. I'd love to get pictures of them."

Stevie shrugged. "Well, all right," she said a little grudgingly. Then her face brightened. "Actually, who says we can't do both?" she said. "While we're looking at the other horses, we can also be keeping a lookout for Duncan Gibbs. And maybe we can talk to people at other stables and try to find out more about him."

"Okay," Carole said. "First we have to find out where the other racers are stabled. Let's go find Judy and ask her."

The vet stepped into the stable shed at that very moment. "Hi, girls," she said when she saw them. "What are you up to?"

"We were just coming to look for you," Carole told her. "Do you know where the other Preakness horses are? We want to go see them."

"Sure," Judy said. She quickly gave them the names and stables of several of the other competitors. Lisa jotted them down in her notebook. "By the way, Max wanted me to give you a message if I saw you. He wants you to meet him back here at noon or a little before to go to lunch."

"Okay," Lisa said, glancing at her watch. "Tell him we'll be here."

The Saddle Club headed for the first stable shed on their list. Inside, they found a restless gray colt named Seattle Skyline. They also found Deborah, who was interviewing the colt's trainer. The Saddle Club waited for her to finish while they watched the horse, who kept tossing his head from side to side, kicking his stall, and doing everything else he could to express his nervous energy. Several grooms did their best to keep him quiet, but to no avail.

"He's always like that before a race," Deborah told the girls as they left the stable together a few minutes later.

"Somehow he can always tell when it's race day, and it gets him all worked up. A lot of people think that's why he doesn't win more often. He uses up all his energy before he even gets near the starting gate." She shrugged. "It's a shame. He has great breeding. His dam is Miss Seattle, the daughter of Seattle Slew, one of the greatest racers in recent history. And his sire is a terrific stakes horse named Sky Over Miami."

"So that's how he got his name?" Lisa asked. "Miss Seattle plus Sky Over Miami equals Seattle Skyline? That's neat."

Deborah laughed. "It is kind of neat. A lot of Thoroughbreds get their names that way."

"What are Monk's parents' names?" Stevie asked curiously.

"His mother was Bright Penny, and his father was Organ Grinder," Deborah said. "Get it?"

Stevie and Carole looked a little puzzled, but Lisa smiled. "I do. Organ grinders are those old-fashioned street musicians who used to have performing monkeys. And bright means the same as shiny."

"Right. And there you have it: Monkeyshines," Deborah said. "Racehorses' names don't always combine both parents' names—sometimes they don't even use one. But it's fun when they do."

By this time the group had reached the stable of the next racer on the girls' list. It turned out that Deborah wanted to ask the horse's owner a few questions, so she accompanied the girls inside.

"Well, well," an unpleasant voice greeted them. "If it isn't the hotshot Washington reporter and her troop of Girl Scouts." It was Kent Calhoun. He was standing just inside the entrance, talking to a small man who looked like a jockey.

"Hello, Kent," Deborah replied coldly. She turned to the little man. "Is your boss around? I'd like to ask him a few questions."

The jockey directed her to the small office at the end of the aisle and Deborah turned to go. "I'll see you later, girls," she told The Saddle Club. "Enjoy yourselves."

As soon as she'd disappeared into the office, Carole turned to her friends. "I think we'd enjoy ourselves a lot more somewhere else, if you know what I mean," she said, glancing at Kent.

Stevie and Lisa nodded, and the three friends turned to leave.

"Aw, leaving so soon?" Kent called after them sarcastically. But the girls didn't wait to answer.

Once outside, Lisa looked at her list. "I think the next stable is back that way," she said, pointing. "Way at the end of the row closest to the paddock." The girls knew from their previous experience at the racetrack that the paddock was where the horses were saddled before each race. It was located between the stable area and the public area, so spectators from the grandstand and the club-house could come to watch.

The crowds of people were thinner at this end of the stable area. "I guess there aren't as many horses stabled here right now," Carole guessed.

"I guess—hey!" Stevie interrupted herself. "Look! Isn't that Eddie?"

Sure enough, the girls saw the groom hurrying along about twenty yards in front of them. He was glancing around in the same furtive, nervous way they'd noticed earlier.

"What should we do?" Carole whispered.

"Follow him, of course!" Stevie replied. She quickly moved from the middle of the path to one side, under the shadows of the buildings, motioning for Carole and Lisa to do the same. Then the girls crept forward after Eddie, being careful to keep a safe distance behind him so they wouldn't be spotted.

To the girls' surprise, Eddie headed past the last stable building and walked straight toward the paddock. He un-latched the gate and disappeared inside.

"Why is he going in there?" Lisa wondered. "There's no reason to be there this far ahead of the first race."

"Not unless you're up to no good," Carole said.

"Come on. Let's get closer," Stevie said. "We have to find out what he's doing."

The three girls looked around carefully to make sure

nobody was watching. Then they tiptoed over to the paddock fence and peered in.

Stevie gasped when she saw the scene inside. "It's Kelly Kennemere!" she whispered loudly.

Carole and Lisa just nodded, their eyes riveted on the scene in front of them. Eddie and Kelly were standing together just inside the paddock. They were deep in what looked like an intense conversation. Eddie was talking quickly, waving his hands in the air, while Kelly kept shaking her head, looking upset.

Lisa raised her camera and focused. She snapped three or four pictures of the pair.

"I wish we could hear what they're saying," Carole said.

"We don't have to," Stevie replied. "They must be talking about Monkeyshines. Maybe Eddie is explaining why the poisoning trick didn't work."

"Shh! I think they're leaving," Carole warned.

The Saddle Club scooted behind a nearby shrub and watched as Eddie and Kelly walked to the gate, looked around, and then hurried off in different directions.

"Wow," Stevie said as the girls began heading slowly back to the stable area. "I guess that just about proves it. Eddie is guilty. He's in cahoots with Kelly, and maybe her father too, to keep Monk out of the race."

Lisa shook her head. "What we just saw doesn't really prove anything, Stevie," she pointed out. "All we saw was a couple of people talking."

"Oh, come on," Stevie said in exasperation. "Don't tell me you're still not convinced there's something strange going on here!"

Lisa chewed her lower lip for a moment. "I'm almost convinced," she said at last. "There are just too many suspicious things happening for all of it to be a coincidence. But the truth is, we still don't have any real evidence—not evidence that the police or someone would accept anyway."

"Lisa's right," Carole said. "We have to find a way to prove that Eddie and Kelly were the ones who tried to poison Monkeyshines."

"That's going to be tough to do before post time," Lisa said doubtfully.

"But we have to do it," Stevie said stubbornly. "We have to—"

"Hey, look," Carole interrupted. "It's Duncan Gibbs!"

Stevie turned to see the disgruntled jockey stalking about nearby, hands once again shoved deep in his pockets. "Come on, let's follow him," she said.

"Why? I thought we'd decided Kelly and Eddie did it," Carole said, watching as Duncan disappeared around the corner of the next barn.

Stevie shrugged. "Well, like you guys said, we haven't proved anything yet. We've still got to keep our eye on everyone."

They headed in the direction Duncan Gibbs had disappeared. As soon as they turned the corner, though, they had to stop short to avoid running into him. The jockey was standing still, talking to the reporter Kent Calhoun.

"I don't have anything to say about the Preakness," Duncan was growling when the girls came upon him. "I'm not riding in it, am I?"

"I know that," Kent said smoothly. "I was just wondering if you had any thoughts on Monkeyshines—you know, how it feels to know you might have ridden one of the favorites in today's big race?"

Duncan's tanned face flushed a deep red, and he scowled even harder. "I don't have any thoughts on that," he said hotly. "I haven't ridden for that lousy, no-good McLeod in months, and I never will again. He's a petty, stuck-up jerk who has no business being at the track. Aside from that, I have no comment on anything." He shoved Kent aside and hurried away without another word.

Kent Calhoun made a few notes on his pad and strolled away without noticing The Saddle Club.

"Wow," Carole breathed when both men were gone. "Duncan sure sounded mad!"

"You can't really blame him," Lisa said. "Kent Calhoun was being sort of obnoxious."

Stevie shook her head. "No, there was more to it than that," she said. "Duncan definitely sounded as though he had something to hide. And he's obviously still mad at

Mr. McLeod—did you hear the way he was talking about him?"

"So what are you saying?" Carole asked. "You think Duncan is guilty, *and* you think Kelly and Eddie are guilty?"

"It's possible," Stevie said, looking thoughtful. "The more we learn, the more it makes sense. It's like a whole criminal ring or something." She snapped her fingers. "So what we should be doing is going after the mastermind."

"The mastermind?" Lisa repeated skeptically. "Who's that?"

Stevie shrugged. "Mr. Kennemere, of course."

BEFORE STEVIE COULD dash off in search of Garamond's owner, Lisa brought her down to earth again by reminding her that it was almost time to meet Max for lunch. Stevie grumbled as they began the walk back to Mr. McLeod's stable. She was sure they were on the verge of cracking the case.

Carole wasn't so sure. She was convinced that there was some kind of foul play involved, but she thought it was more likely that the disgruntled jockey Duncan Gibbs was behind it than any of their other suspects. Eddie just seemed too nice, and it seemed unlikely the Kennemeres would take such a risk, no matter how unfriendly Kelly Kennemere was.

Lisa, on the other hand, was still trying to work the

87

whole thing out logically. And she had just come up with a logical snag in Stevie's conspiracy theory.

"Hey, Stevie," she said. "Remember what Stephen was telling us about the odds on Monk and Garamond?"

"Some of it," Stevie said. "I didn't really understand all of what he was talking about."

"I think I did," Lisa said. "And I think part of what he was saying was that if a horse is expected to do well in a certain race—like Monk and Garamond are expected to do well in the Preakness—people don't make very much money from betting on them."

Stevie shrugged. "So what? We're not old enough to bet on Monk anyway."

"No, but it means that it wouldn't make sense for anyone to want Monk out of the race so they could bet on Garamond, because they wouldn't make very much money that way," Lisa said.

Stevie's face fell. "Oh." She thought back over what Stephen had said. She still wasn't sure she understood how it all worked, but she trusted Lisa on that sort of thing.

"But wait," Carole said. "There's more money than just bets at stake, at least for the horses' owners." She thought for a moment, trying to remember what Max had told them in the car the day before. "There's a big cash bonus if a horse wins all three races in the Triple Crown. Garamond has already won the Kentucky Derby. . . ."

"Oh!" Stevie gasped. "And maybe Mr. Kennemere

wants to guarantee that he'll win the other two races as well! It all makes sense now. He wants Monkeyshines out of the way because he's too much competition."

"I guess that does make sense," Lisa admitted. "Although if that's the case, maybe we should tell Max or Mr. McLeod and let them handle it."

"No way," Stevie said. "There's no time. It would take days to convince them that we're not just imagining things—"

"Especially since *I'm* not totally convinced myself," Lisa mumbled under her breath.

"—and anyway, we probably have a better chance than anyone of solving the whole thing," Stevie went on. "All we have to do is find Mr. Kennemere and ask him a few penetrating questions and try to get him to reveal something incriminating. He'll never suspect someone like us is on to him."

They stopped in front of Mr. McLeod's barn. "How do we know Mr. Kennemere is even here today?" Carole said.

"He's here," Stevie said confidently. "He's got to be. His horse is running in the Preakness."

Max walked up just in time to hear Stevie's comment. "Who's here?" he asked.

Stevie gave him a guilty smile. "Oh, hi, Max," she said. "We were just wondering if Garamond's owner came to see him race."

89

"Of course he did," Max said. "Deborah just went to interview him."

"Oh, good," Stevie said without thinking. Seeing Max's suspicious look, she quickly added, "So when's lunch? I'm starving." She didn't want Max to know what they were up to—especially since both he and Judy seemed convinced that the moldy-hay incident had been an accident.

"We can go right now if you want," Max said. "That way we'll have plenty of time to eat and get back to the track for the first race. One of the grooms told me about a terrific little diner not far from here."

"On the way there, could we look for a one-hour photo shop?" Lisa asked. "I've already used up two rolls of film, and I'd love to get them developed right away."

"Sure thing," Max said. "Let's go!"

WHEN THE SADDLE Club and Max returned to the track, the first thing they noticed was the crowd. If they had thought there were a lot of people around in the morning, they could hardly believe how many were here now. The grandstand was swarming with spectators of every description, from grizzled old men with cigars in their mouths, to tourists in Hawaiian shirts, to young women outfitted in new spring dresses and fancy hats. It was crowded and noisy and very exciting. The Pine Hollow group made their way through the throng to a little stand where a woman was selling programs. Max bought one for each of the girls, then led them through the grandstand to the clubhouse, where Mr. McLeod had a reserved box of seats.

"Whew," Carole said once they were seated. "It's a real mob scene out there. I never imagined so many people came to the racetrack!"

Lisa didn't answer. She was already taking pictures, trying to capture the sight of the colorful crowd, the lush green infield, the fluttering flags, and everything else about the festive scene.

Stevie, meanwhile, was scanning the other boxes around them. "Hey, Max," she said a little too casually. "Do you happen to know what Mr. Kennemere looks like?"

Max looked up from his program and shrugged. "No. But I do know he has a horse running in the second race." He pointed to the page in front of him.

Stevie looked where he was pointing. Max had the program open to the page that listed the entries for the second race. That much Stevie could figure out. But aside from that she couldn't make hide nor hair of the jumble of information printed in tiny letters in the boxes containing the horses' names. "How can you tell that?" she asked.

"If you know how to read it, the program tells you practically everything about each race and the horses in it," Max told her. Carole leaned over to listen, and even Lisa put down her camera. "At the top of the page, here,"

Max went on, "the name, distance, and conditions of the race are listed." He flipped back a page. "For instance, here's the first race, which we're about to see. It's a maiden race."

"Does that mean it's for young girl horses?" Carole asked with a giggle.

Max smiled. "Not exactly. It means that only horses that have never won a race can enter. As it happens though, this race is restricted to mares and fillies three years of age or older. The distance they'll be running is a mile and a sixteenth. See? Here's where they tell you that, and here's where they list the amount of the purse and the weight the horses will be carrying."

"What about all the stuff listed for each horse?" Lisa asked. "What does all that mean?"

Max flipped to the page for the Preakness, which was the eighth race. "Let's use Monkeyshines as an example," he said. "Look at the line right here under his name."

The girls peered at it. It read "Dk. B. c. Organ Grinder —Bright Penny by Minimum Wage."

"I know Organ Grinder and Bright Penny are his parents, and Minimum Wage must be his grandfather," Stevie said. "But the rest of it makes no sense."

"The Dk. B. stands for his color—dark bay," Max said. "And 'c' means colt, as opposed to 'f' for filly, 'g' for gelding, 'h' for horse—that's a stallion—or 'm' for mare."

"What about all the other stuff?" Lisa asked, scanning the rest of the entry.

"It tells you all kinds of things," Max said. "There's Mr. McLeod, listed as owner, and the names of the jockey and trainer. Here you can see how much weight the horse will be carrying in the race, and his predicted odds, as well as a description of the jockey's silks. And here you can see where the horse was bred and by whom, how many times he's raced, and where he placed in each of those previous starts, as well as how much money he's won, and the times of his latest morning workouts."

Carole shook her head, amazed at the amount of information packed into the tiny space. She began paging through her program, examining the lists of horses entered in each race and trying to make sense of all the information.

She flipped back to the listings for the first race. As soon as she did, a familiar name jumped out at her, and she gasped. She elbowed Stevie in the ribs and pointed.

"Duncan Gibbs!" Stevie exclaimed. "He's riding in the first race!"

"Who's Duncan Gibbs?" Max asked.

"Oh, he's just a jockey we met," Stevie explained quickly. "Stephen knows him."

Luckily Max didn't question them any further—it was time for the start of the race. Cheers rang out from the crowd as the horses emerged onto the track for the post parade, before warming up and heading for the starting gate. Everyone in the place seemed to be having a good time, and The Saddle Club was no exception. They forgot all about moldy hay and mysterious motives as the horses warmed up and then were loaded into the starting gate. A few seconds later the horses were in the gate, a bell rang, and the race began. Stevie, Carole, and Lisa cheered as loudly as anyone. Lisa took a few pictures of the race, although she was afraid that she was too far away to get any really good shots.

When it was over, they watched the winning horse stand in the winner's circle to have its picture taken. They also noticed with some satisfaction that Duncan Gibbs's mount had come in last. After discussing the race with Max for a few minutes, the girls remembered their mission and excused themselves, saying they wanted to walk around and see the sights.

"All right," Max said. "Just be sure to meet back here before the fourth race. That's the one Hold Fast is in."

"We'll be here," Stevie promised. Then The Saddle Club left the box and made their way to the top level of the clubhouse stands, where they could see all the seats below them.

"Now what?" Carole asked. "We still don't know what Mr. Kennemere looks like."

"Besides, if he has a horse running in the next race, he's probably in the paddock or somewhere," Lisa pointed out.

"Wrong," Stevie said triumphantly. She had just spotted Kelly Kennemere's blond head in a box not far from where the girls were standing. Sitting beside Kelly was a

94

portly, balding man in his fifties. "That must be him right there."

She started down the steps toward the box, but Lisa put out a hand to stop her. "I really don't think we should bother him right now," she said. "The race starts in less than ten minutes. Let's try to talk to him afterward."

"Well, all right," Stevie said. "But you'd better hope his horse doesn't win, or he'll disappear down to the winner's circle and we'll lose our chance."

The Saddle Club wandered around the clubhouse for the few minutes remaining, then went back outside to watch the race. Mr. Kennemere's horse didn't win, but it came in second.

"Come on," Stevie said, heading toward the Kennemeres' box.

Carole and Lisa exchanged nervous glances and followed.

When they reached the box, Mr. Kennemere was chattering excitedly to his daughter about the race. Kelly was nodding and smiling.

"She's actually very pretty when she smiles, isn't she?" Lisa observed to Carole in a whisper.

Meanwhile Stevie had stepped up to Mr. Kennemere's seat and cleared her throat. Mr. Kennemere looked up at her expectantly, a happy expression on his genial face. "Yes? What can I do for you, young lady?" he asked in a deep, booming voice with a touch of a southern accent.

"Hi there, Mr. Kennemere. We're friends of Mr.

McLeod's, and—" Stevie stopped and bit her lip, annoyed with herself. She hadn't meant to say anything to let him know they were connected with Monkeyshines, at least not right away. Now Mr. Kennemere might have his guard up and be less likely to say something incriminating. She decided just to continue, hoping he hadn't heard her.

But he had. "David McLeod!" Mr. Kennemere shouted cheerfully. "How is that old rascal doing? I haven't seen him since the Derby! I can't wait to see him today after the Preakness—from my spot in the winner's circle, that is!" He grinned and elbowed his daughter, who smiled weakly. Stevie noticed that Kelly, for one, didn't seem pleased to see The Saddle Club.

That gave her added confidence, and she pressed on. "Well, anyway, we just wanted to come over and congratulate you on your horse coming in second just now."

"Why, thank you, young lady." Mr. Kennemere beamed at her. "He's a fine colt. We have high hopes for him."

Stevie moved a little closer, staring into his eyes. "Although you probably would have liked it better if he had come in first, right? You probably don't like to have your horses come in second, do you?"

Mr. Kennemere let out a laugh, as deep and booming as his voice. "Well, sure I'd like it if my horses won every time, honey!" he exclaimed. "But racing just doesn't work that way, I'm afraid." He gave Stevie a wink and a grin. "Just ask your pal David McLeod about that, eh? Ask him how he liked coming in second to my colt in the Derby!" He burst out laughing again.

"Um . . ." Stevie thought fast. She had the sinking feeling that she was losing control of this conversation. She had to get Mr. Kennemere talking about the upcoming race. There was no time to be subtle. "So, then, how do you think you'll feel if Garamond loses to Monkeyshines today?" she asked.

Mr. Kennemere stopped laughing and assumed a serious expression, though the girls could still see a twinkle in his eye. "Well, now, that would be a shame," he said. "You see, David and I have a little private bet on today's race, don't we, sweetheart?" He nudged Kelly again, and she nodded.

"A private bet?" Lisa said. "What is it?"

"Well, I suppose it would be all right if I told you." Mr. Kennemere leaned a little closer. "Whoever loses has to dress up in a butler's uniform and serve refreshments at the winner's victory party!" He chuckled again, and even Kelly smiled a little.

Carole smiled too. It was hard to picture the serious and dignified Mr. McLeod dressed up as a servant, carrying a tray of appetizers. She had the funniest feeling that the bet had been Mr. Kennemere's idea. And she also had the feeling that this jolly, friendly man couldn't possibly be behind any sort of plot against Monkeyshines.

However, Stevie hadn't given up yet. "So you'd really be upset if Monkeyshines were to win, right?"

"Upset? Of course I'd be upset!" Mr. Kennemere roared good-naturedly. "I'd miss out on the chance to see David scurrying around in a penguin suit!"

"No," Stevie said frantically, "that's not what I mean. I mean you'd probably even be willing to do something to make sure your horse wins the race."

Mr. Kennemere looked puzzled. "I'm not sure what you're driving at, honey. Of course I do everything I can to make sure my horses are ready to race—doesn't everyone?"

"No, no, that's not what I mean. I mean you might even consider, um, having someone do something to Monkeyshines—maybe even feed him some moldy hay to make him sick before the race," Stevie said. As soon as the words had left her mouth, Stevie wished she could take them back. She had meant to question Mr. Kennemere so subtly that he'd have no idea it was happening —not blurt out their suspicions point-blank.

Carole and Lisa gaped. They couldn't believe Stevie had just blurted out their suspicions either. They turned to Mr. Kennemere, wondering if he would react angrily.

But he just continued to look confused. "Moldy hay?" he repeated. "What in the great green world are you talking about, sweetheart? Who's been eating moldy hay?"

Stevie stared at her feet, her face red. "Uh, we found some in Monkeyshines's stall this morning. We thought someone in your barn might have had something to do with it," she mumbled, wishing she could sink through the floor.

Mr. Kennemere was shaking his head, looking concerned. "Monkeyshines ate some moldy hay?" he asked. "Is he all right?"

"He's fine, sir," Stevie said. She glanced at Kelly out of the corner of her eye and saw that the young woman was frowning. That gave her new determination. Even if Mr. Kennemere didn't know anything about the incident, it didn't necessarily mean his daughter was innocent as well. "We do have reason to think someone connected with Garamond might have been involved though. Maybe even your daughter."

Kelly sat up straighter in her seat, looking startled, but she didn't say anything.

"Oh, really?" Mr. Kennemere said, beginning to smile again. "Let's hear your reasons."

"First of all," Stevie said, "Kelly didn't seem to want us around last night when we went to look at Garamond— especially when she heard we were friends of Mr. McLeod's. Then this morning, after we found the hay, we saw her again, and she seemed really nervous." Stevie paused to let that sink in. "And finally," she continued, "we saw her having a secret meeting with Monkeyshines's groom, who we think might be in cahoots with her."

Carole had been watching Kelly Kennemere carefully

throughout Stevie's speech. The young woman's face had been growing redder and redder with every word, so that in the end she looked as if she were about to explode. Carole raised her eyebrows. Maybe Stevie's suspicions were right!

"Daddy, I have something to tell you," Kelly blurted out suddenly.

The Saddle Club exchanged a triumphant look. She was about to confess!

But the girls were as surprised as Mr. Kennemere at Kelly's next words. "I've got a new boyfriend," she said. "Well, actually not that new—we've been seeing each other for a couple of months now. But I've been keeping it a secret because I wasn't sure you'd approve. He's not the kind of guy I usually date—he didn't even go to college."

"What?" Mr. Kennemere exclaimed. "Who is it, sweetie?"

Kelly took a deep breath. "It's Eddie Hernandez—he's the groom these girls were talking about. We're in love."

Stevie's jaw dropped. Carole gasped. Lisa almost dropped her camera in surprise. "You and Eddie are—a couple?" Stevie stammered.

Kelly nodded. "Sorry to blow your theory. I'm not your horse poisoner. But I *have* been sneaking around. And any contact with people from Maskee Farms makes me nervous, for obvious reasons." She turned to her father. "Just today Eddie was trying to convince me that it was

100

time to stop hiding our relationship." She glanced at The Saddle Club. "I guess that's when these girls saw us. But I was just so afraid you'd be mad, Daddy."

By this time Mr. Kennemere had recovered from his initial surprise. For a second his mouth turned down in a frown. "Well, I'll admit I'm a little disappointed—"

"I knew it," Kelly interrupted. "I knew you wouldn't approve!"

"Hold on, sweetheart," Mr. Kennemere said. "You didn't let me finish. I'm disappointed only that you kept this from me." His face broke into a wide smile. "But how could I be mad that my only daughter is in love? And with an honest and hardworking fellow like young Hernandez, no less?"

"Really?" Kelly said. "You approve of Eddie even though he's only a groom? You really do?"

"Of course!" Mr. Kennemere boomed. "I've known the young man for some time now—through David McLeod, of course. He swears by Eddie Hernandez—after all, he trusts him completely with Monkeyshines." He paused. "But how did you meet him, Kelly?"

"We met when I flew down to Hialeah to visit you for my spring break," Kelly explained. "Eddie was there with Monkeyshines then." She looked over at The Saddle Club and smiled. "Hialeah is a racetrack in Florida," she explained. "And by the way, thanks for your snooping. I guess I underestimated my father."

"I guess you did, my dear!" Mr. Kennemere said with a

grin. "But never mind. This is wonderful news. Just wonderful." He reached out to give his daughter a hug. The Saddle Club watched, feeling a little touched in spite of themselves.

The tender moment was interrupted by a loud nasal voice from the aisle. It was Kent Calhoun, the reporter. "Excuse me, Mr. Kennemere," he said loudly. "Could I have a word with you about the Preakness?"

"Come on," Carole whispered to her friends. "I think that's our cue to leave." The Saddle Club crept away as Kent Calhoun began to question Mr. Kennemere about Garamond's chances.

"WELL, SO MUCH for most of our suspects," Stevie exclaimed in disgust when the girls were back inside the clubhouse. "It wasn't Mr. Kennemere, *or* Kelly Kennemere, *or* Eddie."

"I'm glad it wasn't Eddie," Carole said. "I always knew he was too nice to be a horse poisoner."

"Me too," Lisa agreed. "But we do still have one suspect left, and he's not so nice."

"Duncan Gibbs," Stevie said with a nod. "It has to be him."

"But how can we prove it?" Carole said. She pulled her program out of her pocket and flipped through it. "He's riding in three or four other races today. He won't have time to do anything suspicious."

Stevie thought for a second. "I have an idea. Let's go

talk to some of the other jockeys. They must know Duncan pretty well. Maybe one of them can give us some clues. Maybe he even told one of them about his plot."

Carole and Lisa shrugged. Stevie's plan sounded a little farfetched, but they couldn't think of anything better to suggest.

They walked to the stable area, showing their special passes. After the frenzy of the stands, the stable area seemed relatively peaceful. The girls took up a position outside the jockeys' room just beyond the paddock and waited for someone to come out.

They didn't have long to wait. Less than five minutes later a small, wiry, red-haired man came out of the building. Stevie hurried forward to meet him.

"Hi there," she said brightly, giving him what she hoped was a dazzling smile. "My name's Stevie."

The jockey, who was a couple of inches shorter than Stevie, looked up at her. "Hi yourself, Miss Stevie," he replied. "I'm John."

"Hi, John," Stevie said quickly. "Um, do you by any chance know a jockey named Duncan Gibbs?"

"Know him?" John said. "Sure, I know him. He's a buddy of mine. Why're you asking?"

Stevie shrugged. "No reason," she said. "We just wanted to ask you a few questions about him."

John grinned. "No problem, missy," he said. "Let me see if I can guess what particular information you're after.

Duncan is twenty-four years old, five foot two, and no, he's not married." He winked at the girls.

For a second Stevie was confused. Then she realized what John was talking about—he thought they had a crush on Duncan! "No, you don't understand," she said urgently. "That's not the kind of questions I meant. We need some more specific information—"

"Oh, I get it," John interrupted, still grinning. "You probably knew all that other stuff from the newspaper, right? Well, if you need to know anything more detailed than that, maybe you'd better talk to Duncan yourselves. If you're lucky, maybe he'll even give you his autograph." He winked again and walked away.

Stevie sighed in frustration. "This isn't getting us anywhere," she exclaimed.

In the distance, Lisa heard the track loudspeaker announce the post parade for the third race. She cleared her throat. "Stevie? Maybe it's time to give up," she suggested tentatively.

"Give up?" Stevie cried. "The Saddle Club never gives up! Besides, we're closer than ever to solving this mystery!"

"But we don't have much time," Lisa said.

"It doesn't matter," Carole said. "Stevie's right, Lisa. We've narrowed down our list of suspects. All we have to do is find a way to prove that Duncan is guilty. We can't let him get away with trying to poison Monkeyshines."

"What?" came an outraged cry from very close behind them.

The three girls whirled around and found themselves face-to-face with Duncan Gibbs, who was accompanied by the red-haired jockey John.

"What's all this about Monkeyshines?" Duncan demanded. He had obviously overheard what Carole had just said.

Stevie faced him bravely, hands on her hips. "We found moldy hay in his stall this morning," she said. "We think you put it there to make him sick, because of your fight with Mr. McLeod."

"You're crazy, little girl," Duncan snarled. "I did no such thing."

"But we saw you near his stall—" Carole began to say.

Duncan cut her off with a look. "Listen, you junior Nancy Drews, or whatever you are," he growled. "I may not like McLeod much, and I have my reasons for that. But no matter what I might like to do to him, there's no way I'd ever take it out on a great colt like Monkeyshines." He was quiet for a moment, and his expression softened a little. "That horse was one of the best I ever rode," he added in a low voice.

Stevie, Carole, and Lisa exchanged glances. Duncan sounded sincere. But for all they knew, it could just be an act.

"Look, girls," John put in, stepping forward. "I have no idea what this is all about, but I can tell you one thing.

Duncan is as honest as the day is long. He'd never do anything illegal or unethical, especially if it involved hurting a horse."

"Don't waste your breath, John," Duncan snapped, whirling around and beginning to stalk away. "Let's get out of here." The two men disappeared into the jockeys' room.

Just then Stephen, Mr. McLeod's jockey, walked toward the girls from the opposite direction. "Well, hello there," he greeted them with a smile. "How are you enjoying your day at the track?"

"Stephen, how well do you know Duncan Gibbs?" Stevie asked the jockey, not bothering to answer his question.

"Duncan? Weren't you asking about him earlier today?"

"We sure were," Carole said. She glanced at Stevie and Lisa. "I think we ought to tell him why."

Her friends nodded. The Saddle Club proceeded to tell Stephen the whole story. When they'd finished, he just shook his head.

"If there's any bad guy to be found, I can tell you one thing for sure—it isn't Duncan Gibbs," the jockey said.

"But you were just telling us how much he hates Mr. McLeod, so we thought—" Stevie began to say.

Stephen didn't let her finish. "Like I was also telling you, Duncan is a bad-tempered, stubborn blowhard who sometimes thinks he knows better than the trainers he works for. That's cost him some jobs, not to mention some friends," Stephen said. "But he's no criminal, and he really does love the horses he rides. He'd never do anything to hurt them."

Stevie, Carole, and Lisa glanced at one another again, unconvinced.

"If you don't believe that, then at least you can believe this," Stephen said. "You say you found that hay around seven this morning, right?"

The girls nodded.

"Well, I was in the track cafeteria having breakfast this morning from around twenty of seven to about five after," Stephen said. "And Duncan Gibbs was there the whole time I was, reading the newspaper. He couldn't have been skulking around Monk's stable planting bad hay."

"But what other explanation is there?" Stevie exclaimed, unwilling to lose their last suspect.

Stephen shrugged. "The explanation is, there's no explanation. It must have been an accident." He glanced at his watch. "Whoops, I'd better get inside if I don't want to be late. Hold Fast and I are in the next race, you know."

"We know," Lisa said. "We'll be cheering for you."

The girls waved good-bye as the jockey headed in to get changed. Then they wandered aimlessly back around the paddock toward the gate to the clubhouse.

After a few minutes of silence, Stevie spoke up halfheartedly. "You know, we don't really know Stephen all that well," she said. "Maybe he's covering up for Duncan. . . ."

Seeing the looks on her friends' faces, she let her voice trail off. Stephen wasn't covering up for Duncan, and Stevie knew it. She sighed. After all their work, she couldn't believe they were no closer to solving the mystery than when they had started.

"You know, I'm beginning to think Stephen is right," Carole said quietly. "I think it must have been an accident after all."

Stevie shook her head. "I still can't believe it," she said with a frown. "Something just doesn't seem quite right about it—there are too many coincidences that don't make sense."

"Maybe," Lisa said, "but we're fresh out of suspects."

"And motives," Carole added.

Stevie shrugged and sighed. "I guess you're right," she admitted. "But I really wish we could get to the bottom of it."

"Come on," Lisa said. "Let's go back to our seats. It's almost time for the next race."

The Saddle Club rejoined Max in the box. Mr. McLeod and Judy were there too. The three adults were discussing Hold Fast's chances and didn't notice the girls' glum expressions.

Lisa rested her chin in her hands and stared ahead moodily, waiting for the race to start. The more she thought about it, the more she thought Stevie was right.

The moldy-hay incident was just a little too suspicious to be written off as an accident. Even though she hadn't been that interested in the investigation at first, she couldn't help thinking that now they seemed to be giving up, and that meant they'd failed. It wasn't like The Saddle Club to fail at anything—and it certainly wasn't like Lisa. She didn't like the feeling.

To take her mind off it, she picked up her camera and started fiddling with the focus, aiming it at different people in the crowd. Then, when the horses stepped onto the track for the post parade, she focused on them. But she was so far away that she could recognize Hold Fast only by Stephen's blue and white silks. She snapped a picture anyway. It turned out to be the last one on the roll, and Lisa barely had time to put in a new one before the race started.

It was an exciting race, and The Saddle Club cheered loyally for Hold Fast, but they weren't feeling quite as enthusiastic as they had earlier in the day. Somehow just being at the track didn't seem quite as exciting to them anymore—even when Hold Fast finished third.

"What now?" asked Carole after the race was over.

As Lisa tucked her roll of used film into her bag, she remembered the pictures she'd taken to the developer before lunch. "My film should be ready by now," she said. "How about if we run and pick it up?"

Carole glanced at her watch. "Okay," she agreed. "We have a good hour and a half before the Preakness."

Stevie nodded, perking up a little. "No matter how much we kid you about this photography stuff, I can't wait to see the pictures," she said. "I hope you got some good ones of Monkeyshines."

The Saddle Club quickly told Max and Judy where they were going. Then they headed for the track entrance.

"HERE YOU GO," the clerk at the photo shop said, handing Lisa several thick packets.

"Thanks." Lisa paid her bill, then she and her friends left the shop.

"Okay, let's see them," Stevie urged once they were outside on the sidewalk. "Open them now."

"All right, just a second," Lisa said. She carefully slit open one of the envelopes and pulled out the first batch. Stevie and Carole crowded closer so they could look at the pictures over Lisa's shoulders.

"Oh! There's a good one of Garamond," Carole said admiringly as Lisa flipped slowly through the pile.

Stevie nodded. "And check out that one of Judy by the track entrance," she said. "Some of these are really good, Lisa!"

"I guess all that practicing is paying off," Carole commented.

"Practice makes perfect," Lisa said with a grin.

Meanwhile Stevie was staring at the next picture.

"Hey, look, it's Blackie! This one turned out really well —you can see every detail."

"It's true," Carole said. "I think this is the best one yet." Suddenly she frowned, and leaned a little closer. "Hey, isn't that that reporter in the background?"

Stevie and Lisa looked closer too.

"You're right." Lisa squinted at the tiny figure that could just be seen at the edge of the picture. It was Kent Calhoun, and he was leaving the Maskee Farms stable. "What's he doing there?"

"I don't know," Carole said. "I didn't notice him there when you were taking the picture."

"He almost looks as though he doesn't *want* to be noticed," Stevie said. "See how he's sort of peeking out? Like he doesn't want anyone outside to see him leaving."

Carole gasped. "You're right!" she exclaimed. "Do you know what this means? He could have been the one who tried to poison Monk!"

"Of course!" Stevie cried. "Why else would he be skulking around Mr. McLeod's barn at that time of the morning?"

Lisa rolled her eyes. "Well, let's see," she said. "He could have been looking for Mr. McLeod to interview him. Or he could have been looking for Stephen to interview him. Or Eddie, or Judy, or the trainer, or any of half a dozen other people."

"No way," Stevie declared. "He's guilty. I can feel it in my bones." She grabbed the photo out of Lisa's hand and waved it in the air. "And we have the evidence right here."

Carole shook her head. "I'm not sure about this, Stevie. What possible motive could Kent have? Besides, the picture isn't evidence. All it shows is a man walking out of a stable shed. There's no law against that."

"Come on, you guys," Stevie said. "Don't tell me you're not just a tiny bit convinced that Kent might have done it."

Lisa shrugged. "I'm not convinced either way," she said. "He was there at around the right time—the picture *does* prove that. But just because he was there doesn't mean he did it."

"What it *does* mean is that we've just got to do a little more investigating," Stevie said eagerly. "Even if his evil plot failed, we still can't just let him get away with it!"

Carole looked doubtful. "We don't have much time. The Preakness starts in a little over an hour, and we'll probably leave pretty soon after that."

"Then we'll have to come up with a good plan," Stevie declared. "Come on, we can talk about it on our way back to the track. We've got a horse poisoner to catch!"

10

"I DIDN'T THINK any more people could squeeze their way into this place," Carole gasped as the three girls shoved their way through the grandstand a few minutes later. "But they did!"

It was true. The racetrack was packed to the eaves with people, all eager to see the exciting showdown between Garamond and Monkeyshines. It was so crowded that The Saddle Club could hardly move.

"How are we ever going to find Kent Calhoun in this mob scene?" Lisa asked, dodging to avoid a baby carriage. She breathed a sigh of relief as they finally reached the entrance to the clubhouse. It was a little less crowded there, though not much.

"We'll have to split up," Stevie decided. "It's the only way." She glanced around. "I'll go back out to the grandstand and look there. Lisa, why don't you stay here in the clubhouse, and Carole, you can search the stable area."

"What do we do if we find him?" Carole asked.

Stevie shrugged. "I don't know," she said. "Just use your instincts. We'll meet in twenty minutes by those phones over there." She pointed to a bank of phones near the door leading out to the paddock area. Then she hurried off before Lisa or Carole could say another word.

"If I thought any of us might actually find him, I'd be worried," Lisa said to Carole, looking at the throngs of people milling around them. "But what are the odds of locating one person in this mess?"

"Pretty slim," Carole said. "Especially if we have only twenty minutes. Still, we have to try, for Monk's sake."

EXACTLY TWENTY MINUTES later, after a fruitless search of the clubhouse, Lisa made her way back to the spot by the phones. While looking for Kent she had encountered Mr. McLeod, Mr. Kennemere, Max, and Deborah. But Kent Calhoun was nowhere to be found.

Lisa looked around the meeting spot, which was much more deserted than it had been earlier. She guessed most people were either in the stands, waiting to watch the race, or in line to place bets. Neither Stevie nor Carole had returned yet. Then Lisa spotted a familiar face, and froze. It was Kent Calhoun, talking on one of the phones!

Lisa looked around again, wishing frantically that her friends would show up quickly. The last thing she wanted to do was face Kent alone. Nervously, she fingered the packet of photos in her pocket. As long as Kent was on the phone, Lisa decided, she didn't need to do anything. She just hoped Stevie and Carole arrived before Kent finished his conversation.

In the meantime, that conversation was becoming audible to Lisa, because Kent's voice had grown louder in the few seconds she'd been standing nearby. It sounded to Lisa as though Kent were arguing with someone, although the subject of the dispute wasn't clear.

"But if I just had a little more time," Kent was saying, "there's a colt in the tenth that I know can bring it home. It's a sure thing. And he's a real long shot—the morning line had him at forty to one."

Lisa's eyes widened as she remembered what Stephen had told them earlier. Kent was obviously discussing the odds on a horse in the tenth race. He must be talking about gambling!

"Then I'll have your money, and more," Kent went on. "And that should make up for . . ." His voice trailed off as he turned and noticed Lisa watching him. His face darkened, and he continued to speak quickly and quietly into the phone for a few seconds, and then hung up.

Lisa backed away a few steps, feeling a little frightened. She wasn't sure what she'd just heard, but she had a feeling it meant trouble. She gulped nervously and looked around once more for Stevie and Carole, but they were still nowhere in sight.

Kent walked up to her. "What's the big idea, kid?" he demanded harshly. "Don't you have anything better to do than listen in on other people's private conversations?"

"Oh, uh, I wasn't listening," Lisa fibbed. "I was just waiting to talk to you about, um, about Monkeyshines."

"What about him?"

"Well, we—that is, my friends and I—think that someone may have wanted to keep him from running today," Lisa said, trying to keep her voice steady. No matter how nervous she was, she knew she had to do her best to carry out Stevie's plan. The Saddle Club was depending on her. Monkeyshines was depending on her too.

Kent shrugged. "What does that have to do with me?"

"That's what we'd like to know," Lisa said. She paused for a second, feeling a little pleased with herself. That sounded just like something Stevie might have said! Then she continued. "We have reason to believe you might know something about it."

Kent looked startled for a split second, but he quickly regained his composure. "I have no idea what you're talking about," he said calmly. "And I don't have time to waste talking to a bunch of weird schoolgirls with overactive imaginations. I have work to do." He shook his head. "Honestly, sometimes I wonder why they allow children to come to the track at all."

Lisa couldn't believe how rude he was being. Schoolgirls, indeed! She was so angry that she forgot completely about being nervous. "Oh, yeah?" she snapped. "Well, if that's the case, you won't mind if we show our evidence to the police!" She grabbed the incriminating photograph out of her pocket and waved it in front of him.

"Evidence?" Kent said. Before Lisa could react, he snatched the picture out of her hand and looked at it. Then he laughed. "This is your evidence? What does this show? It shows me, a well-known track reporter, walking out of the shed where one of the Preakness favorites is stabled." He laughed again. "Ooh, the plot thickens— maybe I'll even *write a story* about Monkeyshines! Wouldn't *that* be suspicious?"

Then he smirked. "But I wouldn't want any little girl's crazy accusations, however unfounded, to ruin my reputation. So I think I'll just take care of your 'evidence' right now." Before Lisa could move to stop him, he ripped the picture in half. Then he ripped the halves again and dropped them into the trash bin by the phones. He laughed again, loudly and unpleasantly.

Lisa was angry at herself for letting him snatch the picture, but she was even angrier at him. How could he just laugh and crack jokes after the terrible thing he'd tried to do to Monkeyshines? "Fine," she said hotly. "You're right. We can't really prove anything, even with that picture. But we know you tried to poison Monkeyshines. You wanted to hurt that sweet, beautiful horse. And in my opinion, that makes you a pretty rotten person." She put her hands on her hips. "Wouldn't you have felt guilty if he'd gotten really sick because of what you did—maybe even died?"

"What do you know, you stupid kid," Kent said, sneering. "There wasn't enough of that bad hay to kill him, or even make him really sick. There was just enough to make him colicky enough so—" He caught himself and stopped speaking.

"Colicky enough so he wouldn't be able to run?" Lisa demanded. "Why would anybody want to be such a bad sport and ruin the race for everybody?"

Kent leaned forward and grasped Lisa by the arm, his fingers digging into her skin. "You don't know anything about it," he snarled. "You just don't realize—racing is big business, and there's a lot of money at stake. You couldn't possibly understand—"

"No, but I think I could," a voice rang out.

Kent gasped and dropped Lisa's arm. Lisa, just as startled, turned to see Mr. McLeod standing behind her. Max and Deborah were with him.

"Max! Mr. McLeod! Deborah!" Lisa exclaimed. "Where did you come from?"

"We were just on our way out to the paddock to meet Monkeyshines," Max said. "We saw you and came over to see if you wanted to join us."

"That's right," Mr. McLeod added, frowning and looking very stern. "But we arrived just in time to overhear some of your very interesting conversation with Mr. Calhoun."

119

Kent started to back away. "Listen, I can explain," he began. "I'm not sure what you think you heard, but—"

"We heard enough for me to do this," Mr. McLeod said. He stepped over, picked up one of the phones, and punched in a few numbers. He identified himself to whoever answered, then requested that track security send someone over right away.

"I'm telling you, you're making a big mistake," Kent said frantically. "I didn't do anything wrong! It was all a setup!"

Mr. McLeod gave him a withering look. "Tell it to someone else, Calhoun," he said disgustedly. "You're a disgrace to a great sport."

Deborah had been scribbling wildly on her notepad. Now she stepped forward, the microphone to her small portable tape recorder in hand. "Mr. Calhoun, do you have any statement you'd like to make at this time?" she asked, holding the microphone up to his face.

He tried to swat it away. "Leave me alone," he shouted. "I don't want to talk to you."

But when the security guards arrived a moment later and took Kent away, Deborah followed, still questioning him. Max watched her go, a grin on his face. "Now, that's what I call poetic justice," he declared.

Mr. McLeod turned to Lisa. "I want to thank you, young lady," he said. "How on earth did you figure out that that man tried to poison my horse?"

"Well, Stevie and Carole were really the ones who

were suspicious after we found the moldy hay," Lisa admitted. "But they finally convinced me." She gave the two men a brief summary of The Saddle Club's investigation—leaving out a few of the more embarrassing parts, including their conversation with Mr. Kennemere. "And then, when we saw the picture, we finally figured out who it must have been," she finished.

Mr. McLeod shook his head. "Eddie told me about that moldy hay, but I thought it must have been an accident. If it hadn't been for you girls, nobody would ever have been the wiser!"

"Hey, what's going on?" came a voice behind them. It was Stevie. She and Carole had just arrived on the scene. "Sorry we're late," Stevie added.

Lisa grinned at her friends. "Boy, are you ever!" she said, raising her camera to capture the perplexed look on their faces.

LISA LEANED ON the paddock fence with her friends and watched as the horses entered in the Preakness walked around the ring, stretching their legs in preparation for the race. Monkeyshines looked more beautiful than ever, his perfectly groomed coat shining in the late afternoon sunlight. Eddie, who was leading the colt while Stephen conferred with the trainer, grinned and winked at the girls as he passed.

"I still can't believe we missed the whole thing," Stevie repeated for about the tenth time.

"I can't believe you did either," Lisa said. "I was scared to death."

Max and Judy walked over just in time to hear her comment. "I'm not surprised," Judy said. "You girls really should have spoken to Max or me or another adult about your suspicions."

"That's right," Max agreed. "You had no idea what kind of maniac you could have been dealing with! You're just lucky this Calhoun fellow wasn't violent."

"Sorry, Max," Carole said contritely. "We were afraid you wouldn't have believed us. Everyone else was so sure it was an accident."

Just then Mr. McLeod walked up to the group, accompanied by several men in suits. "Hello there," Mr. McLeod said. "These gentlemen are track officials. They're interested in speaking to the young ladies who solved our mystery."

The track officials introduced themselves and then asked to hear Lisa's version of what happened. She told them as quickly as she could, aware that it was getting close to post time. After all this, the last thing she wanted was to miss the chance to see Monkeyshines run.

When she finished, the officials nodded, seeming satisfied. Then one of them glanced at the others and grinned. "You know," he said, "we've already found out that this young lady is quite a photographer." He gestured at Lisa. "And now that Calhoun is out of action, his press pass is free. . . ."

One of his companions nodded. "True," he said. He turned to Lisa. "How would you like to see what it's like to be a track photographer for this race? You'll be able to watch at close range—right down at track level, by the finish line."

Lisa gasped. "*Would* I!" she exclaimed. "That'd be great! I'll be able to get some really exciting shots that way!"

"Way to go, Lisa!" Carole said, giving her friend a pat on the back. "Just don't forget us when you win the Pulitzer Prize."

Lisa looked at her friends anxiously. "Oh! You don't mind, do you?" she whispered. "I mean, maybe we could talk them into letting all of us—"

Stevie shook her head firmly. "You earned this fair and square," she said. "You were the one who took the picture, nabbed Kent in the end, *and* got him to confess."

Carole nodded in agreement. "Just promise to give us copies of the pictures you take down there."

Lisa smiled at her friends. "It's a promise," she said. "Thanks, guys. You're the best friends in the whole world."

"We know," Stevie said matter-of-factly.

Just then an outrider—the mounted track worker who would lead the racers onto the track—called, "Riders up!" The Saddle Club watched as Eddie gave Stephen a leg up and the jockey swung into the saddle.

"Come on," one of the officials said to Lisa. "I'll take you out to the track now so you can get in position." Lisa nodded and followed as he hurried off.

"We'd better get moving too," Max told Stevie and

Carole. "If we hurry, we can make it back to our seats in time to catch most of the post parade."

Stevie, Carole, Max, Judy, and Mr. McLeod were in their seats in Mr. McLeod's box by the time the horses passed in front of the grandstand for the first time. All around them, people were cheering for their favorites and calling to the jockeys.

"Look at Monk!" Carole said, elbowing Stevie in the ribs. "Doesn't he look beautiful?"

"He sure does," Stevie said. The colt was stepping along proudly, his neck arched gracefully. "They all look beautiful."

"You know, we've spent so much time today trying to solve that mystery, I've hardly even thought about the race," Carole admitted. "I can't believe it's about to start —we're about to watch the Preakness!"

"I know," Stevie said. "Isn't it great?"

They watched as the lead ponies moved away and the racehorses began to warm up. Stephen urged Monkey-shines into a brisk canter. The colt tossed his head, seeming to enjoy the exercise and the roar of the crowd. The other horses were also trotting, cantering, or galloping, stretching out their long legs. A few minutes later they had turned around and were making their way back along the track toward the great metal starting gate.

"I can hardly stand the suspense," Carole moaned.

"Don't worry," Stevie told her. "Monk will win." But her voice betrayed her own excitement.

"That's what I like to hear," Mr. McLeod said from his seat just behind Stevie.

Max wasn't listening. He was peering down at the track just below them. "Look, isn't that Lisa?" he said, pointing to a tiny figure standing by the inside rail near the finish line.

The others looked. "It is Lisa!" Carole exclaimed.

"And she's got the best seat in the house," Stevie added. She cupped her hands around her mouth. "Lisa!" she shouted. "Lisa! Up here!"

There was no way Lisa could have heard Stevie above the noise of the crowd. But she was looking for her friends too, and soon located Mr. McLeod's box halfway up the stands in the clubhouse. When she saw Stevie and Carole waving frantically, she waved back.

Then she turned back to watch as the horses approached the gate. She wished her friends could be down here with her—as the horses had passed by, she'd been almost close enough to reach out and touch them.

"The horses have reached the starting gate," said the announcer's voice over the loudspeaker.

There were ten horses in the race. Lisa watched as they were led into the narrow stalls of the starting gate one by one. Monkeyshines was the fifth one to go in. Garamond was sixth. There was a slight delay when the eighth horse refused to enter the gate, but after a moment the jockey and the starting assistants managed to coax him in. The

126

last two horses entered quickly, there was a moment of breathless anticipation, and then . . .

"They're off!" the announcer cried.

"Go, Monk!" Stevie and Carole shrieked in one voice.

The horses broke cleanly, leaping forward out of the gate as if they were all one large, many-legged creature. Then some surged forward and some dropped back, until they were running in two groups.

The announcer's voice rang out over the noise of the excited crowd. "Seattle Skyline takes the lead on the rail, followed by Overdrive and Anything Goes, with Tuffy Too just behind. There's a break, and then it's Garamond and Monkeyshines head and head . . ."

As the horses swept around the first turn, Monkeyshines and Garamond matched each other stride for stride. Stevie and Carole watched as the two horses held their positions in the middle of the pack. They guessed that the jockeys were conserving their mounts' strength, waiting for the right moment to ask them for more speed.

"And now, as the horses enter the backstretch, Seattle Skyline holds the lead, and Anything Goes passes Overdrive to take second place. Tuffy Too drops back and is running with Garamond and Monkeyshines. A gap of two lengths, and it's Polly Presto, Laughing Cat, and Montego, with Avondale trailing."

Stevie was hardly listening to the announcer. Her eyes were fixed on Monkeyshines. "Go, Monk, go!" she cried.

Monkeyshines and Garamond held their positions until they reached the final turn. Then they started moving even faster, still matching each other stride for stride. They passed one horse and then another, and by the time they rounded the turn and entered the homestretch, there was no one ahead of them at all. The crowd responded to this with an enthusiastic roar. The announcer's voice rose to a fever pitch as the two horses led the field into the final stretch, still neck and neck, their jockeys urging them to even greater speed.

"Go, Monk! Go!" Carole screamed. She was vaguely aware of Stevie and the others shouting around her, but all her attention was focused on the track.

As Monkeyshines and Garamond thundered down the homestretch toward the finish line, Lisa could hardly tear her eyes away to get her camera ready. But she knew that the finish of this race was one shot she didn't want to miss. She focused carefully, then held her breath. The pounding of approaching hooves was so loud now that it all but drowned out the roar coming from the stands behind her.

Seconds later the horses swept by. Lisa snapped her picture, capturing Monkeyshines crossing the finish line —ahead by a nose!

STEVIE AND CAROLE found Lisa standing by the winner's circle. An exhausted but still spirited Monkeyshines was inside, posing proudly with a blanket of black-eyed Susans, the traditional prize of the Preakness, draped over his shoulders. Stephen was grinning at the camera as Mr. McLeod accepted a large trophy and tried to answer all the questions that television reporters were asking him.

"Wasn't that a great race?" Lisa asked her friends when they reached her. She was still a little breathless from the experience of seeing the racers pass so close in front of her.

"It sure was! Monk was wonderful," Carole said. "Although Garamond gave him a run for his money."

"They're both wonderful," Stevie declared. Now that her horse had won, she could afford to be generous. "Did you get your picture?"

"Yup," Lisa said. "And I'm about to get another one. Hey, Max!"

Max, who was standing nearby, heard her and came over. Lisa handed him her camera.

"Could you get a picture of the three of us?" she said.

Max looked surprised. "You want *me* to take your picture?" he asked. "With *your* fancy new camera?"

Lisa nodded and put her arms around her friends' shoulders. "Being a photographer is fun, but I want at least one picture of the three of us."

"Fair enough," Max said, raising the camera and quickly adjusting the focus. "Say 'winner's circle'!"

"Winner's circle!" The Saddle Club chorused, and Max snapped a picture of them standing in front of the winner's circle containing Monkeyshines, the winner of the Preakness.

12

THREE SATURDAYS LATER The Saddle Club was gathered in front of the television set at Carole's house. The Belmont Stakes, the third race in the Triple Crown, was due to start in a few minutes, and the girls were watching the live TV coverage from Belmont Park in New York.

"I still think we could have talked our parents into taking us to New York if we'd tried a little harder," Stevie commented, stuffing a handful of popcorn into her mouth.

Carole laughed. "I don't know about that, Stevie. I think we were pretty lucky to make it to the Preakness— and that was a lot closer to home."

"That was really a fun day, wasn't it?" Lisa said, her eyes on the TV as the camera panned across the excited crowd in the grandstand.

"You can say that again," Stevie said.

"Although I can still hardly believe that Kent Calhoun was willing to poison Monk just to pay off his gambling debt," Carole said.

Stevie nodded. "I guess he must really have owed a lot of money," she said. She knew how that felt—she usually owed one or another of her three brothers at least a month's allowance. But she also knew that even if she owed them each a million dollars, she would never do anything as awful as what Kent Calhoun had done. "It's horrible to think that anyone would ask him to do that— or to think that he actually would try."

"Definitely," Lisa said. "It's horrible to think people like that even exist."

"But it makes me glad we were able to figure out that Kent was the one who did it," Carole said. "At least we know he won't ever have the chance to try something like that again. And the punishment fits the crime. People like him shouldn't even be allowed near a horse, or any other animal for that matter." A few days after the Preakness, Mr. McLeod had called the girls to tell them that Kent Calhoun had been barred from the track for life—he couldn't set foot on Pimlico or any other racetrack in the country ever again. Mr. McLeod had decided not to press criminal charges against the reporter. He figured that Kent's being barred was punishment enough. Mr. McLeod had also insisted on giving Lisa a cash reward for solving the mystery of the moldy hay. Naturally, she split it three ways, since the whole Saddle Club had really done the solving. The girls had celebrated by spending part of the money on the three hugest sundaes they could stomach at TD's, the local ice cream shop. Then they had allowed their parents to put the rest of the money in the bank for them—for a rainy day, as Mrs. Lake had put it.

"One other good thing did come out of the whole incident, you know," Lisa pointed out. "Deborah got the scoop of the year by being there for Kent's capture—in addition to the great story she wrote on the race itself."

"True." Carole nodded. "Max said that gained her a lot of respect among the other race journalists." She grinned. "As it turned out, none of them like Kent much either."

"Big surprise," Stevie said. "I'm sure nobody will miss Kent Calhoun at the track. He was a creep even when he wasn't doing anything illegal."

"That's for sure," Lisa agreed. "Still, even though we met one or two bad people at the track, we met an awful lot of nice people too."

"You mean like Mr. Kennemere, for instance?" Carole said. "I'm still embarrassed about suspecting him like we did. He turned out to be a great person." Mr. Kennemere, along with a lot of others, had sought out The Saddle Club after the race to congratulate them once he'd heard about what had happened.

"It still seems a little weird that he thanked us for saving the horse that beat his horse," Stevie said. "Especially since it meant he'd have to pay up on that bet and play butler at Mr. McLeod's victory party." She couldn't help grinning at the thought of portly Mr. Kennemere squeezed into a butler's uniform, carrying a tray of drinks.

"I don't think so," Carole replied. "You heard what he said. He was glad it was a fair race. That made perfect sense to me." She shrugged. "You know, the first time I went to the racetrack, I was really surprised when I found out how concerned everybody seemed to be about making money. I wasn't used to thinking of horses that way, and it made me a little uncomfortable. It even made me think the racetrack might not be such a great place, even though there were horses there."

Her friends nodded, waiting for her to continue.

"But now I know that racing means more than just money to a lot of people," Carole went on. "People like Mr. Kennemere."

"And Mr. McLeod," Lisa added. "And Eddie, and Stephen. Like Max told us all along, racing is a way of life for a whole lot of people like them. It *is* how they make money, but it's also what they love to do."

"It's an interesting way of life too," Carole said, still thinking about everything she had learned during her day at Pimlico. "It's different from anything we're used to, all right, but it does have to do with horses, and that automatically makes it interesting. And Max and Deborah weren't kidding when they kept talking about all the history and everything. There's a lot to learn about racing, even if you already know a lot about horses."

"Still, I wouldn't trade places with any of them," Stevie said loyally. "I like Pine Hollow the best."

Her friends laughed and agreed. They all watched the TV screen as the horses came out onto the track to begin the post parade.

"The bottom line is, horses are great no matter what they do," Carole said as she watched Monkeyshines prance proudly in front of the crowded grandstand. "And Monk is definitely one of the greatest I've ever known— aside from Starlight, of course."

"That's for sure," Lisa said. "Monk's a real celebrity. I'm glad we got to meet him." She gave her friends a sidelong glance and grinned. "And I'm glad I got plenty of pictures to help us remember it."

They all laughed at that, including Lisa. After she'd gotten all her film back from the developer, she had counted the pictures she'd taken on Preakness day. She had used up all seven rolls of film that she'd brought. She had exactly fourteen pictures of Blackie, more than thirty of Carole and Stevie standing beside various horses throughout the stable area, including Garamond and Hold Fast—and forty-seven of Monkeyshines. She had also gotten some very good pictures of the Preakness it-self, and, as promised, she had had copies of those made for each of her friends. She also made them copies of the picture of Blackie with Kent in the background. He had torn up the print, but she still had the negative. And she knew that that was one photo they would all want to keep as a memento of their exciting day—along with the great picture of The Saddle Club posing in the winner's circle.

A few minutes later the horses were in the starting gate. The bell rang, the doors flew open, and the TV announcer cried, "And they're off!"

This time there were only seven horses running. Monkeyshines and Garamond were near the back of the field as the horses rounded the clubhouse turn. But by the middle of the long backstretch Garamond had taken the lead, and Monkeyshines was only a couple of lengths behind him. At the top of the stretch they were once again neck and neck, and their closest competitor was five lengths behind. As they pounded down the homestretch, they pulled farther and farther away from the other horses, until it was as if they were the only two horses in the race. The sleek, beautiful Thoroughbreds ran as they had never run before, their great muscles straining, but neither could seem to pull even half an inch ahead of the other. They swept across the finish line, still running so close together that the girls couldn't tell which of the flying legs belonged to which horse.

Stevie let out the breath she'd been holding. "Who won?" she asked. "I couldn't tell."

"I couldn't either," Lisa said.

Just then the TV flashed the words "photo finish."

"That means it was so close that the judges have to look at a photograph of the finish to decide the winner," Carole said, remembering the fact from one of her books.

The girls waited, fidgeting with suspense. Finally, endless moments later, the TV announcer said, "The winner of the Belmont Stakes is—Monkeyshines!"

"Yay, Monk!" The Saddle Club cried in one voice.

ABOUT THE AUTHOR

Bonnie Bryant is the author of more than sixty books for young readers, including novelizations of movie hits such as *Teenage Mutant Ninja Turtles*® and *Honey, I Blew Up the Kid*, written under her married name, B. B. Hiller.

Ms. Bryant began writing The Saddle Club in 1986. Although she had done some riding before that, she intensified her studies then, and found herself learning right along with her characters Stevie, Carole, and Lisa. She claims they are all much better riders than she is.

Ms. Bryant was born and raised in New York City. She lives in Greenwich Village with her two sons.

Saddle Up For Fun!
Join The Saddle Club

As an official Saddle Club member you'll get:

- *Saddle Club newsletter*
- *Saddle Club membership card*
- *Saddle Club bookmark*
- *and exciting updates on everything that's happening with your favorite series.*

Bantam Doubleday Dell Books for Young Readers
Saddle Club Membership Box BK
1540 Broadway
New York, NY 10036

SKYLARK

Bantam Doubleday Dell
Books for Young Readers

Name _____

Address _____

City _____ **State** ___ **Zip** ___

Date of birth _____

BFYR - 8/93